WOOF!

THE NEVER-ENDING TALE

Based on the Central Independent Television Series

by Terrance Dicks

PUFFIN BOOKS

PUFFIN BOOKS

Published by the Penguin Group
Penguin Books Ltd, 27 Wrights Lane, London W8 5TZ, England
Penguin Books USA Inc., 375 Hudson Street, New York, New York 10014, USA
Penguin Books Australia Ltd, Ringwood, Victoria, Australia
Penguin Books Canada Ltd, 10 Alcorn Avenue, Toronto, Ontario, Canada M4V 3B2
Penguin Books (NZ) Ltd, 182–190 Wairau Road, Auckland 10, New Zealand

Penguin Books Ltd, Registered Offices: Harmondsworth, Middlesex, England

First published in Puffin Books 1994
10 9 8 7 6 5 4 3 2 1

The moral right of the author has been asserted

Typeset by Datix International Limited, Bungay, Suffolk
Made and printed in Great Britain by Clays Ltd, St Ives plc
Set in 12/13pt Monophoto Baskerville

CONTENTS

The Milkman Never Rings Twice

It was very early in the morning in a quiet suburban street.

A milk float glided gently along the road and stopped outside a house. Before the milkman could get down to make his delivery, a shaggy little dog jumped down from the float. Just as the dog reached the corner a furious barking broke out. The dog paused, cocked its head, then went on its way.

It scampered along the road till it came to the park gates. Just as it arrived, the park keeper was opening the gates for the day and the little dog trotted through. It passed through the empty playground, climbed the steps to the slide and whizzed down the other side.

It ran happily across the grass until it reached the gate on the other side of the park. Just as it arrived, the park keeper turned up on his bicycle, opening the gates for it to go out.

It made its way through the empty morning streets till it reached the town centre. It trotted along the still-empty high street, pausing occasionally to check out a particularly interesting window display – a model shop, a sports shop or a video store.

After a while it turned off the high street and went along a back street until it reached the rear entrance of a hotel.

Through the door came the clatter of the busy hotel kitchen. A couple of white-coated chefs were drinking tea and enjoying the morning air. One of them saw the dog and patted it on the head. 'Hello, boy, haven't seen you for a while. Like something to eat?'

'Woof!'

'I'd give you some milk, but the milkman's very late today.'

'Shall I find him an old bone?' said the other chef.

'He's not keen on bones. See if there's some strawberry shortcake left . . .'

'Woof!' said the dog.

The chef laughed. 'That dog understands every word I say!'

Comfortably full of strawberry shortcake, the dog went on with its early-morning walk, finishing up in front of a sports shop. It ran down a side alley, jumped on to a dustbin, from there to a wall, and from the wall to a bathroom extension roof. It ran up one side of the roof and down the other, and took a flying leap through an open bedroom window.

Just as the dog landed in the room, there was a knock on the bedroom door. A man's voice called, 'Come on, Rex, you don't want to be late for school!'

The dog grabbed the end of the duvet in its teeth, dragged it off the bed and jumped into a dog basket – just as the door opened. Mr Thomas glanced into the room, saw the disarrayed bed, and concluded that his son, Rex, was already up.

'Must be in the bathroom. Good lad!'

He went away. The little dog started scratching . . .

In case you're wondering what all this was about, the scratching was a warning that Rex Thomas was about to turn from a dog back into a boy. Turning from a boy to a dog and back again was just something that happened to him from time to time.

Michael Tully, his best friend, was in on the secret. A boy who turns into a dog needs a human helper . . .

Mr Thomas was making Rex's sandwiches when Michael Tully tapped on the door and came in.

'Morning, Mr Thomas.'

'Morning, Michael. Rex isn't down yet, but he shouldn't be long. I'd offer you a cup of tea, but we've run out of milk and the milkman's late today.' Mr Thomas looked at his watch. 'You're early, aren't you?'

'My sister Eileen's in charge at home. She didn't want us to be late for school so she got us all up at five.'

'Where are your parents?'

'Uncle Pete won a holiday for four in Corfu, so he and Auntie May took Mum and Dad with them.'

Rex came into the kitchen. 'Hi, Michael!'

'No cereal I'm afraid,' said Mr Thomas. 'No milk!'

'We didn't get any milk either,' said Michael. 'Eileen poured fizzy orange on ours.'

'It's all right, Dad,' Rex said hurriedly. 'I woke up very early so I had something then.'

Mr Thomas finished the sandwiches and passed them over to Rex.

'I've been thinking, it's time that dog had a name.'

Rex jumped. 'Which dog?'

Mr Thomas sighed. 'There's only one dog around here, Rex. It seems all wrong just calling him "the dog" all the time.'

Rex smiled. 'I'm sure he doesn't mind!'

'I mean, I know he's only a stray,' said Mr Thomas,

'but he does spend a lot of time here. I thought it would be nice if he had a name.'

'Good idea,' said Michael.

'How about Teddy?' said Mr Thomas.

Rex looked horrified. '*Teddy?*'

'He looks a bit like an old teddy bear, all cute and cuddly. What do you think, Michael?'

Michael hid a grin. 'I'm not sure . . .'

'I think he should have a name like Sabre,' said Rex. 'Or Silver . . . or Flint!'

Michael burst out laughing '*Flint?*'

'Let's get him in here,' Mr Thomas suggested. 'See what seems to suit him.'

'I don't think he's here,' Rex said hastily.

'Yes, he is. I saw him in your room, in his basket.'

Michael tried to be helpful. 'I thought I saw him run out when you let me in.'

'So did I!' said Rex.

'You were in the bathroom.'

'I saw him through the window.'

'There isn't a window in the bathroom!'

Rex grabbed his schoolbag. 'Anyway, I think we should be going, we don't want to be late for school.'

'Not when we're so early,' said Michael.

They hurried away.

'Your dad's right, you know,' said Michael as they walked to school. 'About the name . . .'

Rex shuddered. '*Teddy?*'

'He doesn't know why he's right, but he's right. If you think about it, it'd be safer. You don't want people finding out about you, do you? And it's pretty suspicious having a boy and a super-intelligent dog, both with the same name living in the same house.'

Rex nodded. 'Yes, all right. But *not* Teddy!'

They turned into the school playground and saw their teacher, Mrs Jessop, directing a sort of chain gang of children, who were staggering towards the bike sheds carrying milk crates.

Mrs Jessop promptly press-ganged them. 'You two! Come and lend a hand. Take this last milk crate over to the bike sheds.'

They picked up the crate between them and set off, Mrs Jessop walking beside them.

'I don't know what the dairy's thinking about. I tell them we need eight pints, we've had eight pints every day this term, then suddenly they decide we don't have enough. But they don't leave us an extra couple of pints – they leave us a lorry-load!'

Mrs Jessop pointed dramatically to a great stack of milk crates piled up in the shade. 'To make matters worse, they missed *my* house completely. I had to have prune juice on my oatcakes!'

It was the end of the school day, and Rex and Michael were walking home. Rex fished a scrap of paper from his pocket and passed it to Michael.

'I made up a list in Music Appreciation. What do you think?'

Michael studied the list of names. 'Gringo? Rocky? *Terminator?*'

'I didn't want them to sound soppy.'

'They're not soppy, they're dangerous. They'd get you into fights!'

They were walking past a high wooden, fence and Michael screwed up the list and tossed it over.

'There's some good names on that list!' Rex said

indignantly. 'Anyway, you can't just toss litter into people's gardens.'

'Okay, okay,' said Michael, heading for a gate in the fence. 'I'll get it back – then we'll burn it!' He went through the gate. A moment later he called, 'Rex, come here!'

Rex followed him through the gate and found himself in a disused garage area that was overgrown with grass. Just inside stood an empty milk float. It was the one he'd hitched a lift on earlier.

Michael pointed. 'Look!'

To his astonishment Rex saw that the milkman was sitting at the wheel of the float, frozen and motionless, like a waxwork.

'It's my cousin Gary,' Michael whispered. 'Uncle Pete's son. He's filling in while Uncle Pete's on holiday.'

He went up to the motionless milkman.

'What is it, Gary? What's wrong?'

Gary stared wildly at him. 'I'm not going back, not to Number Forty-three! You can't make me!' His voice rose hysterically. 'No, no, get him away from me! Tell Dad, no more milk deliveries . . .'

Michael pulled him gently out of the driving seat and led him away from the milk float.

'Come on, Gary, you come with us . . .'

They were sitting in a little café watching Gary drink his third cup of strong, sweet tea.

'A dog frightened you?' said Michael. 'Did it bite you?'

'Well, not bite exactly,' Gary muttered. 'It – growled. Grrr! Like that!'

'Gary, you haven't blown your chance of becoming a milkman just because a dog growled at you?'

Gary shuddered. 'You should have seen it, it was huge! I couldn't go on.'

'So you dumped all the milk in our school,' said Rex.

'It was the nearest place. I couldn't go back to the dairy with it, they'd know I hadn't done my deliveries. They'd see all the milk on the float.'

'What about all the people who rang the dairy this morning when they didn't get their milk?' Michael asked.

Gary hadn't thought of that – thinking wasn't his strong point.

'People want their milk in the morning,' Rex said gently. 'They need it. That's the point of being a milkman.' He looked at Michael. 'We'd better get the float back.'

'Right.'

Rex turned back to Gary. 'You'd better think of a good excuse so they'll let you work tomorrow.'

Gary shrank back. 'I can't . . . all those dogs . . .'

'It's all right,' said Michael. 'This time we're coming too.'

Next morning at first light Rex and Michael stood waiting outside the dairy gates. A milk-float appeared, with Gary at the wheel.

He drew up beside them. 'They're giving me another chance!'

'Brilliant,' said Michael. 'How did you manage it?'

'I did what you said. I told the boss my driving licence had been captured by aliens.'

'That was a joke!'

'I said I was very sorry,' Gary went on. 'The boss said he was sorry too, sorry it was too late to find anyone else. He said if I made one more mistake he'd kill me and drag my body through the streets behind my own milk float.'

Michael looked at Rex. 'Sounds reasonable to me!'

'Do you think he meant it?' Gary asked nervously.

'Probably,' said Rex. 'Don't worry, we'll be with you to make sure everything's okay.'

'I'm very grateful,' said Gary. 'I'll be fine as long as we don't run into any dogs.'

It was then that Rex started to scratch . . .

It was some time later, and Michael was delivering the milk with only his doggy friend to help him.

'Don't worry, Rex,' he said. 'You couldn't have known you were going to change. Gary's probably better off at home anyway . . .'

Rex trotted up to the next house. The empties had been left in one of those little wire crates. Rex looked at the dial on the side of the crate. The pointer was on the three. He picked up the crate by its carrying handle and brought it back to Michael.

'Woof! Woof! Woof!'

'Three pints, right!' said Michael. He put three bottles in the crate and took it back to the doorstep.

Rex jumped up behind the wheel and pressed the control with his paw. The milk float moved off.

Later that morning Rex and Michael, both exhausted, trailed wearily to school.

'Feels more like going-home time,' said Michael.

'Well, it is for us,' said Rex. 'We've been up for five hours!'

Mrs Jessop cycled up to them. 'Morning, you two! This is a surprise!'

'Is it, miss?'

'I mean, *I* have to come in early to polish my cane and change the straw in the classroom, but it does seem a little early for you two.' She got off her bike and walked along with them.

Michael yawned. 'We woke up early, so we thought we'd come in, miss.'

'You'll be pleased to know the milkman got it right. I think it was a new one.'

Rex and Michael looked at each other.

'What makes you think that, miss?' asked Michael.

'The old one *never* used to wake me up shouting, "Don't drop it, Rex, miss'll kill us!"'

'We were just trying to help out,' said Rex. 'No one was going to get any milk otherwise.'

'I'm sure the dairy can sort it out.'

'I don't know if they can,' said Michael. 'You see, Gary the new milkman's my cousin, and he's scared of dogs. One of them growled at him and he had a sort of collapse.'

'His dad's gone to Corfu,' explained Rex.

'He won a competition, miss, on a cheese packet,' said Michael. 'That's Gary's dad, not Gary.'

'And now he may lose his job,' said Rex.

'That's Gary,' said Michael.

'All right, all right,' said Mrs Jessop. 'I can see something's bothering you both. Why don't you tell me all about it – starting in Corfu and working westwards . . .'

By the time they reached the bike sheds they'd told her the whole story. As usual, Mrs Jessop had the answer. 'Your cousin needs therapy – help to get over his fear. When people are afraid of spiders, you cure them by getting them used to spiders, little by little.'

'And you reckon that would cure him?' asked Rex.

'Undoubtedly!'

'He just needs someone to help him get used to dogs?'

'That's right. Someone with a bit of common sense and ingenuity – and a nice friendly dog, of course.'

'I see,' said Michael. He looked thoughtfully at Rex . . .

It took quite a bit of persuasion to get Gary to try Michael's dog therapy, but eventually he agreed. Now Rex, Michael and Gary were standing outside the Thomas's front door.

'Right,' said Michael. 'Imagine you're delivering milk to this house.'

Gary went and stood unhappily by the door.

'Deliver the milk then,' said Michael.

'I haven't got any.'

'Pretend,' said Rex. 'Go on!'

Rather half-heartedly, Gary mimed delivering milk. Suddenly a dreadful snarl came from behind him.

Gary jumped, realized it was only Rex and managed not to run.

'Well done,' said Michael. 'A very good start.'

'But that's easy,' said Gary. 'Rex is a boy, not a dog.'

Rex started to scratch.

'That's just the first stage,' Michael explained. 'To get you used to the *idea* of dogs.'

'Michael!' called Rex. 'Mike!'

He disappeared round the corner of the house.

'I know he's a boy, not a real dog, see,' Gary persisted.

'Of course he's not a real dog,' said Michael. 'It's just to stop you being frightened.'

'I am not frightened!'

'Tell him, Rex,' said Michael.

But Rex wasn't there. Instead, there was a small shaggy dog.

'Woof!' it said.

Michael and the dog Rex were gazing upwards. They were looking at Gary, who was halfway up a drainpipe.

'I'm not coming down,' Gary called. 'Get Rex back, I'd rather do it pretending with Rex.'

'It's okay, he won't harm you,' said Michael. 'Do come down!'

Eventually Michael managed to coax Gary down. He led him into Mr Thomas's shop.

'Would it be all right if I took my cousin Gary upstairs for a cup of tea?'

Mr Thomas looked at Gary's white face and knocking knees.

'Is he ill?'

'He's just had a bit of a fright,' said Michael. 'He'll be fine.'

'I was not frightened,' Gary muttered.

'You know where everything is,' said Mr Thomas.

Michael took the still-quaking Gary upstairs.

Gary sat at the kitchen table draining his third mug of tea.

Michael passed him a fourth, and started to pour a fifth.

'Thanks,' said Gary. 'Where did that dog spring from?'

'He sort of belongs to Mr Thomas.'

'He looks a bit, well . . .'

'Dangerous?' Michael shook his head. 'Actually he's a retired guide dog, perfect for us. You can practise with him now.'

'Can't we wait for your friend Rex to come back?'

'You're going to have to meet a real dog sooner or later. Look out of the window.'

Gary looked down into the yard and shrank back. 'Aaargh! He's still there. He'll get me!'

'For heaven's sake, Gary! He's down in the yard. You're inside and upstairs.'

Gary sank into a chair. 'Is there another cup of tea?'

Michael gave him another mug and Gary drained it down.

'Now go and have a proper look,' Michael ordered. 'Go on!'

Gary went over to the window, and managed to look out for at least a minute.

'Brilliant!' said Michael. 'Now I think we should go downstairs and look from a bit closer.'

Gary gulped. 'Just one more cuppa?'

'All right,' said Michael wearily. 'Just one more.'

'Make it four sugars this time, could you?'

Michael and Gary walked out into the yard. The little dog was still sitting patiently at the far end. Gary turned to bolt back into the house, but Michael caught his arm and made him stay.

They walked a few steps closer to the dog.

'Well done!' said Michael.

Gary looked pleased.

Inch by inch, Michael persuaded Gary closer to the little dog. At last Gary managed to reach down and stroke the dog's head.

The dog licked his hand.

The next stage was a little more elaborate. Gary did his 'delivering the milk' mime again. Rex, meanwhile, was tied up close by, pretending to be a hostile guard dog. He tugged at the rope and barked and growled and snarled. As soon as the imaginary milk was delivered, he stopped barking and wagged his tail.

The final stage was inspired by one of Michael's favourite films. He remembered how Inspector Clouseau, the bungling French detective, had an oriental manservant who was trained to keep him alert by attacking him unexpectedly. With this in mind, Michael bent down and whispered in Rex's furry ear. Then he took Gary for a walk.

They set off, walking down the street – and suddenly Rex bounded, barking, from behind a hedge.

Gary jumped, but he didn't run.

Soon after they had turned into the high street, Rex leapt out from a doorway.

Gary hardly flinched.

They were walking past the pond in the park when Rex whizzed past them and landed in the water with an almighty splash. Then he climbed out and shook himself, spraying them with water.

Gary just grinned.

Finally, on the other side of the park, Rex dropped, panther-like, out of a tree, landing just in front of them.

Gary bent down and patted his head.

'Rex,' said Michael. 'I think he's got it!'

Gary had to go back to the dairy to tell them he'd be

working next day, so Michael and Rex walked to the
gates with him.

'You'll be all right on your own tomorrow?' Michael
asked. 'We'll come along if you like.'

'No, honest, I'll be fine.'

Michael yawned. 'It is a bit early for me. If you're
sure . . .'

'Woof!' said Rex.

Michael looked down at him. 'You *want* to go with
Gary?'

'Woof!'

Michael turned to Gary. 'He'll come with you if
you like.'

'Smashing! See you then.' Gary headed for the
dairy gates, then paused. 'Oh, and thank your friend
Rex for me, will you?'

As Michael and Rex walked away, they met Mrs
Jessop.

'Not getting permanent milkman's jobs, are you,
you and Rex?'

'No, miss, we've just been giving Gary a bit of
therapy.'

'How's it going?'

'It's finished, miss.'

'Goodness, that was quick.'

Michael grinned. 'We had a special dog therapist.'

Mrs Jessop looked down at the dog. 'So I see.
What's his name?'

'I don't think Mr Thomas has decided yet.'

'Pity they've got a Rex in the house already. Rex is
the traditional name for dogs. Still, you couldn't have
two Rexes in the house, Rex-the-boy and Rex-the-
dog. That'd be too silly.'

'I suppose it would, miss.'

'Of course it would,' said Mrs Jessop firmly.

Early next morning, Gary's milk round was well under way. Whistling cheerfully, he put a crate of empties in the back of the float, patting Rex on the head.

'I'm sure I'll be all right. Still, it's nice to have company.'

'Woof!'

'No dog is ever going to bother *me* again,' said Gary. He picked up a couple of pints and headed for the next house.

Suddenly Rex caught sight of someone waving from one of the ground-floor windows. He jumped down from the float and ran to bar Gary's way.

'It's all right,' said Gary. 'I won't run away, I'm all right. I'm cured.'

Rex grabbed the bottom of Gary's milkman's coat in his teeth and dragged him back towards the house.

The front door opened, revealing a heavily pregnant young woman in a dressing-gown. 'Can you help, please?' she gasped. 'I need to get to hospital.'

Gary's giant brain went into action. 'You're having a baby!'

'*Yes!* Could you call an ambulance, *please*?'

'No need,' said Gary. 'Hospital's just round the corner, I'll have you there in a flash.'

Minutes later, the woman was tucked up in the back of the milk float, propped up on cushions and wrapped in a duvet.

Gary was hunched over the milk-float wheel like a racing-car driver, Rex beside him.

'Hope we don't meet the police,' said Gary. 'I don't want to be pulled in for speeding!'

Rex shook his doggy head and sighed.

Moving at a good fifteen miles an hour, the milk float sped down the road.

Mr Thomas put down his copy of the local paper.

The headline read: 'PINTA HERO!' in capital letters. Underneath, in smaller letters it said, 'I'll call him Gary, says grateful mum.'

'That young milkman did well, didn't he?'

'He certainly did,' said Michael.

'He's Michael's cousin,' said Rex.

'Is he now? Says here he conquered his fear of dogs to become a milkman. The dairy are very pleased with him. By the way, I've thought of a name for our dog.'

Rex gave him a worried look. 'Oh yes?'

'Bob!' said Mr Thomas. 'It seems just right. Bob was the name of my first cricket coach. And we had a parrot called Bob when I was young.'

'Dad! You can't call a dog after a parrot!'

'I don't know why you're so bothered about it,' said Mr Thomas. 'Anyone would think we were changing *your* name . . .'

It was early next morning and the newly named Bob – who still thought of himself as Rex – was hitching a ride on Gary's milk float. He jumped off at the corner, and Gary waved goodbye.

'See you, Bob!'

'Woof!'

As Rex turned the corner, he heard the sound of savage growling. He heard Gary's voice shouting, 'No, stop it!'

He turned and scooted back – to see Gary standing in the driveway of a house. He was holding two snarling terriers by their collars, keeping them apart at arm's length.

'That's enough,' said Gary sternly. 'I will not have biting and snarling on my milk round. Behave yourselves!'

The terriers hung their heads in shame.

The little dog turned and trotted away.

He arrived the park just as the park keeper was opening the gates. 'Morning, Bob!'

He went on through the town centre, ending up at the back door of the hotel kitchen. The chef looked up. 'Hello, boy!' He turned to the sous-chef. 'Do us a favour, see if there's any of that Pavlova left.'

'Sure,' said the sous-chef.

'Milkman been yet?'

'Oh yes, this new lad's very punctual.'

'Good,' said the chef. He looked down at Rex. 'How about a nice bowl of milk then? All right?'

'Woof!' said Rex.

The Great Demento – and Rex

The car whizzed round the corner and pulled up in front of the little theatre. Michael jumped out of the back and Rex got out of the front passenger seat.

'Thanks for the lift, Dad.'

'Sorry we're a bit late. I'd no idea they were going to deliver this afternoon.'

'Don't worry,' Rex said cheerfully. 'We'll tell you if it's a really good show, and you can bring us again next week!'

'It's a deal.' Mr Thomas fished a handful of coins from his pocket. 'Here, treat yourself to something in the café afterwards.'

'Thanks, Dad.' Rex took the money and hurried after Michael.

Mr Thomas looked at the big poster outside the theatre. The 'top-of-the-bill' act stood out in giant letters:

THE GREAT DEMENTO AND CYRIL

Mr Thomas drove away.

In the foyer Rex gave the tickets to a dinner-jacketed figure, who jerked his head towards a side door with a sign over it: GRAND CIRCLE.

The circle was full and they had to shuffle apologetically past people who were already seated to reach their seats. They just managed to get settled when the orchestra struck up a jolly tune.

'Made it!' Michael gasped.

The curtain rose on a large lady soprano with the sort of voice that shatters glass.

She was followed by some acrobats, a juggler, a high-wire act, a not-too-funny comedian, and a Spanish knife-throwing act that had customers in the front stalls ducking in fear of their lives.

'If this lot's typical, no wonder the music hall's in trouble,' Michael whispered.

'Hang on,' said Rex. 'It's the Great Demento next. Dad says he's terrific.'

The knife-throwers departed, the front-row customers breathed again, and the theatre curtains closed. The band played an impressive fanfare and the manager's voice came over the tannoy.

'And now the Theatre Royal has great pleasure in presenting . . . The Great Demento – and Cyril!'

Nothing happened.

The band played another fanfare.

The curtains stayed obstinately closed.

The band had just begun yet another fanfare when a man appeared through the gap in the middle of the curtains. He was wearing the traditional evening dress, top hat and cloak of the stage magician. The man waved the band to silence.

In a trembling voice he said, 'Ladies and gentlemen, I have something very . . . very . . .' His voice broke as he sobbed, 'Cyril's dead!'

The Great Demento produced an enormous silk handkerchief and blew his nose noisily. With an effort, he went on, 'Cyril was the best friend a man could have. We shall not see his like again. But he was also a

true professional. I know what Cyril would have
wanted: he'd have wanted me to carry on. So, strike
up the band, Maestro . . .' He sobbed again. 'And on
with the show . . .'

Rex and Michael discussed the show over fizzy drinks
and cakes in the café next door to the theatre.

'Poor man,' said Rex. 'You could see he was really
shattered. That Vanishing Dog trick was what he was
really famous for.'

'I still don't get how he did it.'

'Well, he didn't really, did he?' Rex pointed out. 'I
mean, I know he had to improvise, but the Vanishing
Budgie – well, it's just not the same!'

'I suppose not,' Michael agreed. 'Poor old codger. I
wonder how he'll manage, now Cyril's gone . . .'

The Great Demento looked up nervously as the theatre
manager came into his dressing room. 'How do you
think it went?'

'Not well,' the manager replied heavily.

Demento managed an uneasy laugh. 'Well, you
know, audiences . . . It'll probably go better tomorrow.'

'I don't think so. Not unless you go back to your old
act.'

'How can I? I mean, without Cyril . . .'

'I know it's hard for you, and I'm very sorry. But
I'm going to have to insist that you get the act back
up to scratch by Monday, or . . . well, there'll be a
new act as top of the bill.' The manager sighed. 'It'll
probably have to be the knife-throwers.'

'But where am I going to find a new dog?' Demento
protested. 'Even if I do, it could take months to train
him.'

'I'm sorry. I can only give you till Monday.'

In the café Rex started to scratch.

Michael said, 'You okay, Rex? Is it . . .'

'I'm afraid so.' Rex got up, heading for the toilets at the back of the café. 'Keep an eye on my drink, okay?'

A few minutes later a small, shaggy mongrel with large brown eyes and a short, wagging tail trotted out of the toilet and jumped into Rex's chair. Michael fed him a fancy cake and Rex gave a 'Woof!' of thanks. Michael went to collect Rex's clothes.

The Great Demento came out through the stage door and turned wearily into the high street. As he passed by the café, he caught sight of a dog: it was sitting up in a chair next to a boy. A waitress was serving each of them with a bottle of fizzy drink.

Demento looked on in fascination as the dog began sucking up its drink through a straw. With a sudden surge of hope, he hurried into the café.

He found himself a table in the corner, close enough to watch the dog, and ordered a coffee. He could hear the boy talking to the dog. 'More orange?'

'Woof!'

The boy poured some more orange into the dog's glass. The dog sucked it up through the straw.

The waitress came over to Demento's table. 'Anything else, sir?'

'Amazing!' whispered Demento.

'Pardon?'

'Marvellous!

The waitress smiled. 'Oh, the dog! Yes, he is nice, isn't he? He's called Bob.'

She went over to the dog's table. 'Finished?'

'Yes, thanks,' said Michael.

'You, Bob?'

'Woof!'

Michael stood up. 'Let's go, then.'

They walked over to the cash desk by the door.

Suddenly Michael stopped. 'Hey, you're the one with the money!'

The dog trotted back to the table, picked up a neatly rolled bundle of clothes and brought them back to the boy.

Michael reached into the pocket of the jeans and took out some coins. Tucking the clothes under his arm, he paid the bill. Boy and dog left the shop.

Demento leapt up, called for his bill from the waitress, thrust the money into her hands and hurried after them.

Rex and Michael walked along the high street till they reached Rex's father's shop. They stopped by the side passage that led to the house.

Michael was just telling Rex that he'd leave his clothes in his room when a voice called, 'Excuse me! Excuse me!'

An eccentric-looking old fellow was hurrying up to them.

'Excuse me, but that's a very remarkable dog you have there – remarkably intelligent, I mean!'

'Thank you,' Michael answered politely.

'You probably don't know who I am . . .'

Michael looked hard at him. 'No . . . yes, I do though! You're the Great Demento. We've just been to see your show.'

'Then you know about – my loss?'

'Cyril? Yes, it's really sad.'

'That's why . . . I was wondering if you'd be interested in selling me your dog? He'd be well looked after. Short working hours, his own special corner in my camper, and a good walk every day.'

Michael shook his head. 'No, I'm sorry.'

'I'll give you five hundred pounds for him.'

Michael's eyes widened. 'Pardon?'

'Make it a thousand,' Demento said desperately.

'I'm afraid he's not for sale. Not at any price.'

'I see,' Demento said sadly. 'I'm sorry to have bothered you.'

Mr Thomas was having supper in the kitchen when his son, Rex, came in. 'Sit down, I'll get your supper,' Mr Thomas said. He got up and took a plate of slightly congealed stew from the oven.

Rex sat down and began to eat.

'Did you have a nice time?' his father asked.

'Yes, thanks.'

'How was the Great Demento?'

'All right.'

'Only all right?'

Rex swallowed a mouthful of stew. 'It was all a bit sad, really. His dog died just before the show so he couldn't do his famous Vanishing Dog trick.'

'I suppose he'll get another dog,' Mr Thomas said thoughtfully. 'When he gets it, I'll take you along to see the show again. We could go for my birthday.' He looked around. 'Talking of dogs, where's Bob?'

'Bob?' said Rex. 'Oh, I think he's round at Michael's.'

'Maybe we should leave a bit of stew for him?'

Rex finished cleaning his plate. 'I shouldn't bother, Dad. I think he's already eaten!'

*

It was the next day, and Rex and Michael were wandering along the high street. They passed a fence with a theatre poster stuck on it: 'THE GREAT DEMENTO AND CYRIL'.

'Poor old Demento must be pretty desperate,' said Michael. 'Offering all that money for you, I mean.'

Rex grinned. 'Oh, I think I'm worth it!'

'No, but if he's offering that kind of money, he must be mad keen to get a replacement dog for his act . . . Pity I couldn't sell you really!'

Rex gave him an indignant look. 'Hang on a minute . . .'

'You could have been the new dog he needed, couldn't you?' said Michael. 'You'd have been really good at it.'

'Thanks a lot!'

They continued on their way.

Neither of them noticed that they were being followed by a camper van. The driver wore a large floppy hat and a bushy beard.

Still unaware of their sinister follower, Rex and Michael came to the surgery of the local vet. Mrs Jessop, their teacher, was unloading a couple of cat-boxes from the back of her car.

'Hello, you two! Don't fancy a couple of moggies, do you?'

'Sorry, miss?' Rex said politely.

She held up the cat-boxes so that they could see through the wire-mesh ends. Inside each box crouched a distinctly fed-up-looking cat. 'I'm just seeing if the vet can find them a good home. My next-door neighbour's getting on a bit and she can't look after them properly any more.'

But Rex wasn't listening. He was wriggling unhappily, seized with a sudden urge to scratch. Another transformation was coming on. Rex looked around wildly for shelter.

Mrs Jessop noticed his distress.' Are you okay, Rex?' 'Yes, miss,' said Rex desperately. 'It's just . . .'

Michael had a sudden inspiration. 'It's just that we're late for collecting our dog, miss. They said to get him round the back. 'Bye, miss!'

Rex and Michael rushed down the little alley that led to the vet's back yard, and Mrs Jessop carried her cat-boxes into the vet's surgery.

A few minutes later, Michael came back up the alley with Rex, now in his dog shape, trotting at his heels.

They went on with their walk.

The camper van drove round the corner and moved slowly after them. Suddenly it gathered speed and drove past.

Michael and Rex strolled on down the high street. A few minutes later, they walked past the parked camper van without noticing it. Just beyond the van was a bus stop with a little queue of people waiting. At the end of the queue stood a man with a big hat, a big, bushy beard and an enormous suitcase. Deep in conversation, Michael talking and Rex putting in the odd 'Woof!', boy and dog walked by.

Michael didn't even notice when the bearded man lifted up his suitcase and dropped it over the little dog. When he lifted the case up again, the dog had disappeared.

Michael walked for some little way before he realized that his furry friend was no longer at his heels. He turned to look for him, but Rex the dog was nowhere to be seen. There was only a bearded man with a big suitcase hurrying towards a parked camper van.

A few minutes later the camper van was careering along a back street, the bearded man at the wheel. Beside him on the wide bench seat was a dog's travelling box. Inside the box was the dog Rex.

After a short journey, the camper van drew up in the little car park behind the Theatre Royal. Carrying the dog-box, the bearded man got out of the van and went through the back door of the theatre. He hurried along the back-stage corridor and emerged on to the stage itself.

Beyond the footlights, the deserted theatre was dark and empty. On the stage was a magician's magic cabinet and a few other props. The man took off his hat, his coat and his beard, revealing the face of the Great Demento.

He picked up a dog collar, already attached to an extending lead, and put the collar on the little dog inside the box.

'Easy, boy!' he said gently, and led the dog out of the box.

It stood there, looking at him, head cocked intelligently.

'Now, there's nothing much to learn,' Demento said eagerly. 'You start by going into the cabinet. Come on, good dog!' The dog turned around and sat down with its back to him, its nose in the air.

'Into the cabinet, this way!' said Demento. He grabbed the dog by its collar and pushed it gently inside.

The dog sat down again.

Demento clicked his fingers by its right ear. 'There! Now – turn to your right!'

The dog looked at him. It stood up – and turned to the left.

'No, this way,' said Demento, pointing to the right. 'You're a clever dog, I know you can do it.'

The dog strolled out of the cabinet and collapsed as if playing dead.

'I know why you're doing this,' Demento said sadly. 'You think I shouldn't have kidnapped you, don't you?'

'Woof!' said the dog decidedly.

Demento sighed. 'You're right. I don't know how I thought I could get away with it. It's just that the manager told me, if I don't do the act properly – well, I'm out!'

He knelt beside the dog and took off its collar. The dog sat up and looked at him intelligently, head cocked to one side.

'I was only going to borrow you for a few weeks,' Demento went on. 'Just till I could get another dog. It takes time to train them, you see. They have to walk into the box . . .'

The dog got up and walked into the box.

'Hit the hidden switch when I close the door . . .'

The dog hit the switch with its paw.

'That's it,' said Demento, closing the door. 'You go down through the secret trapdoor, and when I take the box to bits . . .' Demento began dismantling the box. 'You've vanished!'

Demento took away all four sides of the cabinet – and the little dog had indeed disappeared.

'Perfect!' said Demento. 'The audience claps, the band does a drum-roll, you whizz under the stage, up the steps and reappear!'

Demento made a grand gesture towards the wings.

A strange boy walked on, wearing a frilled shirt and a pair of breeches. (Luckily for Rex, there'd been some old pantomime costumes in a hamper under the stage.)

Demento gaped at him. 'Who are you?'

'*Your* dog?' said the Great Demento. 'I thought he belonged to the boy in the café.'

They were sitting in Demento's dressing room.

'That's my friend, Michael. We sort of – share the dog.'

Demento nodded gloomily. 'I suppose you're going to call the police? You've got every right to.'

'No, I thought I might be able to help you,' said Rex. 'I wondered if you'd like to borrow my dog for your show tomorrow . . .'

The Theatre Royal was packed – and the Great Demento's new dog was a wonder. It trotted on stage with Demento's wand in its mouth. It jumped through paper hoops, it balanced balls on the end of its nose, it even walked a little tightrope. For the grand finale, it trotted into the magician's cabinet and disappeared, reappearing mysteriously from the wings.

The audience applauded like mad.

And at the end of the act the dog went down on one front leg, taking its bow with the proud Demento beside it.

The applause raised the roof as the curtain came down. Backstage, Demento turned to his new partner.

'You were wonderful! Can you come back again tomorrow?'

'Woof!' said the dog. It jumped down and trotted away.

It was a busy time. Every day, after school Rex belted

down to the theatre for the early performance. Every night, after the second house, he joined the Great Demento at the stage door giving autographs to their fans. (Rex gave paw prints with the help of a special ink-pad.) As soon as that was over, he sprinted back home again, to get into bed before his dad looked in to say goodnight.

Still, it was only for a week. Saturday night's performance was the most successful ever. On Sunday, when the theatre was closed, Rex went along to make sure they'd taken down the posters for the show.

To his horror, the old posters were still up.

THE GREAT DEMENTO AND CYRIL

(Demento had decided to keep his old dog's name in the act as a kind of tribute.) There were stickers across all the posters.

RETAINED FOR TWO FURTHER WEEKS BY PUBLIC DEMAND!

The bell went at last, bringing Mrs Jessop's Geography class to an end. Tucked away at the back, Rex was dozing quietly. Michael gave him a jab in the ribs and he jerked awake.

The movement attracted Mrs Jessop's eagle eye. 'I didn't notice you had much to say about the high tundra, Rex.'

Rex yawned. 'Well, miss . . .'

'I suggest a good night's sleep before we challenge the complexities of glacial erosion, all right?'

'Yes, miss,' Rex said sleepily.

'You wouldn't be interested in a mynah bird, would you?'

'Sorry, miss?'

'It's my next-door neighbour, Miss Borthwick, again. She's worried she's getting too old to remember to feed him.'

'That French restaurant in the high street might like him,' Michael suggested. 'They used to have one before.'

Mrs Jessop shook her head doubtfully. 'Have to fatten him up first, there's hardly a scrap of meat on him . . .'

It was break time, and Rex and Michael were wandering across the playground. 'They've kept old Demento on for another fortnight,' said Rex. 'That's another I-don't-know-how-many performances!'

'Tell him you can't do it.'

'How can I? He'll lose his job.'

Michael shrugged. 'The longer you stay with him, the less he'll bother about finding a new dog. You're already exhausted. How long do you think Mrs Jessop's going to put up with you dozing off in class?' Michael thought for a moment. 'Maybe *we* could find him a new dog – it can't be that difficult doing tricks.'

Rex's professional pride was hurt. 'It's not as easy as it looks, you know!'

'Then we'll just have to find him an incredibly bright and intelligent dog!'

Suddenly Mrs Jessop appeared and bore down on them. 'You don't know anyone who wants an incredibly bright and intelligent dog, do you?'

They stared at her.

'Only I just rang Mrs Borthwick to tell her I have found a home for the mynah,' Mrs Jessop went on.

'Now she wants me to find someone to take on her poodle.'

'Brilliant, miss!' said Michael, jumping up and down with excitement. 'Now it's just a question of how long it will take to train him!'

Mrs Jessop looked at him in amazement.

Eventually they got things sorted out. Mrs Borthwick's Sinbad, a small, black French poodle, was handed over to Demento to begin its stage career. A few days later, Rex, in his boy shape, went over to the theatre to size up his successor.

He found Demento on stage rehearsing. 'How's it going?'

'Not too bad. We've been working very hard, haven't we, Sinbad? Let's show Rex what we can do. Sit!'

Sinbad sat.

Demento went over to the magician's cabinet.

Sinbad got up and wandered off.

'Right,' said Demento. 'Now where's he gone? Oh, there you are! Sit, Sinbad.'

Sinbad sat.

'Into the cabinet! In you go!'

Reluctantly, Sinbad trotted inside and Demento closed the door. 'Button, Sinbad,' Demento called. 'Press the button!

Frantic barking came from inside the cabinet. There was a loud scratching noise, followed by the sound of splintering wood . . .

A dusty and dishevelled Sinbad suddenly appeared from behind the cabinet and began racing round the stage in frantic circles. He crashed into a table and upset a hamper, releasing a flight of doves into the air.

Demento sighed. 'I'm glad he doesn't have to take

over just yet, aren't you? We've still got quite a way to go!'

Next day, at school, Rex told Michael about the disaster. They were walking along the corridor on their way to the next lesson.

'It was awful,' said Rex. 'He's hardly taught that dog anything. I mean, how much longer can I go on?'

'You're right,' said Michael. 'He's going to take months.'

'And he won't hurry,' said Rex bitterly, 'because he knows I'm going to be there every night!'

Michael hesitated. 'I wouldn't be too sure about that. Not unless you can manage to be on stage and in the audience at the same time!'

'What do you mean?'

'Your dad rang up last night and invited me to his birthday treat. He's taking us to the theatre – to see the Great Demento. Mrs Jessop's coming too. It's supposed to be a surprise. What are you going to do?'

'There's only one thing I *can* do . . .'

Rex the dog usually disappeared as soon as he could after the last performance, but tonight he didn't. To-night he lurked in the car park, waiting until Demento carried Sinbad, in his dog-box, out to the camper van.

When Demento went back into the theatre, Rex jumped into the back of the van and went over to the dog-box. He lifted the fastening-catch with his teeth, the end of the box swung open and Sinbad's black curly head popped out inquisitively.

Rex turned and jumped down from the van, and Sinbad came out of the dog-box and followed him.

They hid behind some dustbins as Demento came

out of the theatre with an armful of props and put them into the van. He closed the rear door, climbed into the driving seat and drove away.

Rex and Sinbad emerged from behind the dustbins and trotted through the still-open stage door. Unseen by the doorman in his alcove, the two little dogs trotted towards the stage.

When they reached the stage, it was in darkness – until Rex trotted over to the prompt corner and flicked on the working lights with his paw.

He looked around and saw the Vanishing Dog cabinet standing in the wings. He jumped up and pushed at it with his front paws, but it was too heavy. He summoned Sinbad with a quiet 'Woof!', and between them the two little dogs rolled the cabinet on to the stage.

When the cabinet was in place, Rex looked keenly at Sinbad and went over and pushed open the door with his nose. Rex went inside. He looked at Sinbad and woofed gently.

The little black dog trotted over and joined him.

'So far so good,' thought Rex . . .

Early next morning, two dogs were trotting along the canal path towards the caravan site where Demento kept his camper van.

Rex stopped outside the camper door and began to whine. After a moment Sinbad joined in. At the sound of movement inside the van, Rex disappeared into the bushes.

The camper door opened, revealing Demento in his pyjamas. He looked down at the little poodle in astonishment. 'I've been looking for you everywhere! How did you get out of that box?' He chuckled. 'Silly

question to ask a magician's dog, eh? Come on in and
have some breakfast.'

Dog and magician disappeared inside the van.

It was later that evening, and the show was well under
way. The Great Demento was sitting in his dressing room, sick with worry, Sinbad stretched out at his
feet.

Demento looked down at the little poodle. 'Where is
he, Sinbad? Where is he?'

Rex was in the circle, looking almost as worried as
Demento.

He leaned over to Michael and whispered, 'I should
never have done it.'

'You had to. Anyway, if it works, all his troubles are
over.'

'And if it doesn't?'

There was a rap on the dressing room door. 'Two
minutes, Mr Demento!'

The Great Demento stood up. 'Well, Sinbad, this is
the end of the line!' He went out, closing the door
behind him.

Sinbad jumped up, pulled down the handle with his
paw, opened the dressing-room door and trotted after
him.

The theatre manager was standing in the wings. He
turned around and beamed happily as Demento ap-
proached him. 'Another full house, Mr Demento!'

'I was wondering if I could have a word,' Demento
whispered. 'It's rather important.'

'Don't tell me,' said the manager. 'You want to use
the new dog.' He looked down and smiled.

Demento looked down as well and saw Sinbad sitting at his feet.

'You don't have to ask my permission,' said the manager. 'When I'm dealing with an artiste who can fill a theatre the way you do, I'm happy to trust his judgement. If you say the dog's ready, Mr Demento, he's ready!' He picked up his microphone. 'Ladies and gentlemen! The Theatre Royal proudly presents ... The Great Demento – and Cyril!'

Looking totally bemused, the Great Demento shuffled on stage, Sinbad at his heels.

There was a great 'Aahh!' of anticipation from the audience.

Taking no chances, Demento picked up the little poodle and put him inside the cabinet. He turned back to the audience. Behind him, the cabinet door opened and Sinbad popped out again.

The audience roared with laughter. Up in the circle, Mr Thomas and Mrs Jessop were laughing as loudly as anyone.

'He's better than ever!' wheezed Mr Thomas.

Rex buried his head in his hands.

On stage, Sinbad gave Demento an offended look, trotted over to the cabinet and jumped in of his own accord. He pulled the door closed behind him.

The audience cheered and clapped.

There was a drum-roll from the orchestra, a final boom and a puff of smoke, and the sides of the cabinet fell away.

Sinbad had disappeared – and no one looked more amazed than the Great Demento!

In the circle, Mr Thomas and Mrs Jessop clapped like mad.

Michael grinned at Rex – and Rex heaved a huge sigh of relief.

On stage, Demento was gesturing towards the wings – and there was no sign of Sinbad! Suddenly, to a huge roar of laughter, Sinbad trotted on from the other side. Alerted by the laughter Demento swung around just in time. Sinbad jumped up into his arms and licked his face.

'Well, I reckon that dog's marvellous,' said Mr Thomas.

'Wasn't he just?' said Mrs Jessop.

Mr Thomas turned to Michael. 'Wasn't Rex saying something about some difficulty with the training?'

Since she'd helped to discover Sinbad, Mrs Jessop took a personal pride in the little poodle's success. 'No problems that I could see. That animal's brilliant!'

'I don't know how Demento does it!' said Mr Thomas admiringly. 'Rex, you know the man . . . how does he do it?'

The only reply was a deep, melodious snore.

Rex was slumped back in his seat. He was fast asleep!

Getting Up Steam

The coach cruised along the dual carriageway, packed with happy kids, in the charge of a cheerful teacher. They were all off on an educational trip – and anything's better than a day in school.

Rex and Michael were sitting at the back of the coach. Michael had a camera round his neck, and he was reading an account of a recent school football match, written in Rex's straggling handwriting.

'Bit short, isn't it?'

'I'm sorry,' said Rex. 'It's a bit difficult being an ace sports reporter when you keep on turning into a dog!'

'Don't worry, we'll just have to pad things out with the netball results.'

'Look out,' said Rex.

Their teacher, Mrs Jessop, who naturally had bagged the front seat, stood up and turned around to rally the troops. Michael grabbed his notebook.

Mrs Jessop's bossy voice rang down the coach. 'We're nearly there now. Make sure you've all got your worksheets and your packed lunches. They'll start by showing us the engine sheds, then we'll have our picnic. After that, they've promised us a ride in one of their steam trains.'

'Can you go a bit slower please, miss?' called Michael, waving his notebook.

'Taking notes, Michael? How very flattering. I didn't know you were so interested in trains.'

'It's just I have to write something for the school paper.'

'Well, mind you don't misquote me,' Mrs Jessop said sternly. 'I'd hate to have to sue you!'

The coach turned off down a side street. Before very long they were pulling up outside an old-fashioned-looking railway station, surrounded by a high wooden fence.

Mrs Jessop bustled everyone out of the coach and marched them across to the station entrance. 'It's very kind of these people to let us visit their station. I want you all on your best behaviour, so lots of "pleases" and "thank yous" from *everyone*.'

A girl at the back put up her hand. 'Please, miss!'

'Yes, we know you can do it, Shelley,' said Mrs Jessop wearily. 'Not now!'

'Please, miss,' persisted Shelley. 'Why's it got "Closed" written on the gate?'

'What!' said Mrs Jessop. She marched up to the gate.

Shelley was right. Under the sign reading 'MIDLAND STEAM PRESERVATION SOCIETY' a handwritten sign said simply 'CLOSED'.

Mrs Jessop rattled the gate. 'This is where they said, the gate with the sign. Unless there's another one . . .'

She marched off round the corner to investigate.

Michael started writing in his notebook. '"Shocked members of class seven learned at the very gates of the Nottingham Steam Railway that their educational visit might be cut short. Baffled students waited while teacher Mrs Jessop . . ."' He broke off. 'How old do you think she is, Rex?'

'No idea. Why?'

'They always put everyone's age in newspaper reports – in brackets after their name.' Michael started writings again.

'"Teacher Mrs Jessop, brackets, whatever, close brackets, went off in search of another entrance . . ."'

Mrs Jessop was marching back towards them, looking cross.

'"But there appeared to be none,"' Michael concluded.

'This is ridiculous!' Mrs Jessop stormed.

Michael's pencil raced across the page. '"'This is ridiculous,' said a clearly upset Mrs Jessop . . ."'

'Stop that, Michael!'

'"'Stop that, Michael,'"' Michael wrote automatically.

'Don't let's be silly,' said Mrs Jessop. 'Come here and make yourself useful.' She pointed to the fence and beckoned to the biggest boy in the class. 'Gary, give Michael a leg-up.'

Gary made a back, then Michael scrambled on to his shoulders and peered over the wall. The station yard seemed deserted.

'What can you see?' called Mrs Jessop.

'Nothing much, miss. There's no one about.'

He jumped down.

'This is most annoying! I booked us in in February, and they confirmed three weeks ago.' Mrs Jessop waved her arms. 'All right, everyone, back on the coach! I'll find a phone box and we'll soon see what's going on!'

At this point Rex started feeling itchy. 'Michael!'

Michael was still scribbling in his notebook. 'Just a sec!'

'Over here!' Rex called urgently

Michael hurried over. Rex was scratching furiously.

'Ah!' Michael said. 'Don't worry, I'll cover for you.'

'How do I get home?' Rex whispered.

'Good point. Right, we need a plan . . .'

Rex nipped around to the back of the coach as Mrs Jessop turned at the doorway. 'Come along, everyone,' she called. 'Quicker we go, the sooner we'll be back.'

As the class started filing on board, Michael raced around to the back of the coach. A small, scruffy mongrel was standing in a pile of Rex's clothes. It looked appealingly at him.

Michael grabbed the clothes and stuffed them into his sports bag. 'If I cause a diversion by pretending to be sick . . .'

Rex cocked his head − then streaked through a hole at the bottom of the station fence.

Mrs Jessop came round the corner of the coach. 'Michael, what are you doing?'

Michael shoved the last of the clothes into his bag. 'Dropped some of my kit. Miss, I feel a bit sick . . .'

'Well, don't you dare do it in the coach,' said Mrs Jessop unsympathetically. 'Now come along, I want to sort things out and then get back here as soon as I can.'

Michael glanced towards the hole in the fence. 'So do I, miss!'

She bustled him into the coach and a moment later it drove away. Rex the dog poked his head through the hole in the fence and watched it go.

He heard a voice behind him. 'Doggie!' it called.

Rex turned and saw a toddler in a romper suit staggering towards him across the station yard. 'So there is someone here,' Rex thought. 'Too late now, though. Better get moving.'

He turned and nipped back through the hole.

'Doggie!' the voice called again.

Rex turned and to his horror saw that the little kid had squeezed through the gap and was staggering after him.

He stopped and waited for the kid to catch up.

'Doggie!' said the toddler happily, giving him a pat on the head that nearly stunned him.

'Now what?' thought Rex. 'Can't leave him out here in the road.' He trotted back to the hole and went through. The toddler followed. When the kid was safely back in the yard, Rex headed for the gap again. The kid followed.

Rex sighed and trotted across the station yard and on to the platform. The toddler staggered happily after him.

Rex walked along the platform, moving slowly so the kid could keep up.

The place was a wreck. Everything was dirty, dusty and broken down, and there was rubbish everywhere. Down the track he could see an ancient steam engine and some grimy-looking carriages.

He passed a deserted waiting room and an empty booking office.

Suddenly a figure appeared round the side of a building at the far end of the platform. It was a white-haired old granny wearing oily railwayman's overalls and an engineer's cap.

She beamed at the sight of the toddler and yelled, 'Arthur! I've found Simon – he's here!'

Rex trotted over to her and sat at her feet, and Simon staggered after him.

The old lady grabbed the toddler and hugged him. 'You little monkey, Simon. We've been worried silly.'

A white-moustached grandad, presumably Arthur, came running along the platform. Rex saw he was wearing exactly the same railwayman's costume as the old lady. 'Where was he, Nora?'

'Must've been down the other end of the yard.'

Arthur pointed to the dog. 'Where's he come from?'

'Don't know, but I think he brought Simon back.'

'Good dog,' said Arthur. He ruffled Simon's hair. 'If we'd lost you, we'd have had some explaining to do!'

The phone in the booking office started ringing, and the old lady said, 'Better answer that, Arthur.'

Arthur went along to the office and Rex followed. The old man picked up the phone. 'Who? Oh, Mrs Jessop! You mean no one told you? I'm afraid there's a bit of a problem . . .'

' . . . and it was a heck of a run home,' said Rex in his room that evening. 'Luckily I didn't change again till I got back!'

Michael nodded. 'And the steam railway people are selling the place?'

'Not them, the Council. The railway lot only rent it.'

'Why don't they buy it themselves?'

Rex shrugged. 'They probably don't have the money.'

'But according to you it's a proper old-fashioned station,' said Michael. 'Couldn't they raise money by showing people round and giving steam-train rides?'

'No, they couldn't – the place is a mess.'

'So why don't they clean it up? It can't be that bad.'

'You haven't seen it!'

'Maybe I should,' said Michael. 'We've got a very short newspaper all of a sudden. I mean, "School Trip Cancelled" isn't much of a story. I could take pictures, show everyone what they missed.'

'Right,' said Rex. 'How do we get in?'

The two boys stood, staring at the still-closed station gates.

'Well,' said Michael, 'they said we could come – so I'm coming! Come on, Rex, give me a leg-up!'

Rex boosted Michael on to the fence, Michael hauled Rex up after him, and they dropped down on the other side. They walked across the railway yard, clambered over the tracks and climbed up on to the platform. The place was as deserted and as dirty as ever – but now there was a sound of clanging coming from the far end. They walked towards it.

The sound led them into a huge, cavernous engine-shed, filled with enormous old steam locomotives, all in a state of disrepair. The clanging was coming from the nearest locomotive of all – because the toddler, Simon, was bashing it with a hammer.

'Hello!' yelled Michael.

An old man in a railwayman's cap popped his head out of the cab. It was Arthur. He looked down at Simon still happily bashing away. 'Like being inside a drums with him doing that,' he grumbled. 'What can I do for you?'

'We rang yesterday afternoon,' said Michael. 'About doing an article on the steam railway. Mr Thomas and Mr Tully.'

'Rex and Michael,' said Rex.

'Newspaper reporters, eh?' said Arthur. 'Thought

you'd be a bit older. Still, never mind, pleased to see you. Nora!'

The old lady came into the engine shed. She went straight over to Simon and took the hammer away from him. 'Been looking everywhere for that, little monkey!

'These gentlemen are the reporters who rang up,' said Arthur.

Nora looked at them. 'Ah. I thought they'd be a little older.'

'Well,' said Arthur. 'Where would you like to begin?'

Rex and Michael looked blankly at him.

Nora came to the rescue. 'I expect you'd like a ride on a steam train, wouldn't you?'

'Yes, please,' said Rex.

'It'll take him about half an hour to get steam up,' said Nora. 'Would you like to go and help?'

'Brilliant!' said Michael.

'Can you take Simon with you, Arthur?' She smiled at the boys. 'He's our daughter's, you know.'

'He's a menace,' Arthur muttered. 'Do I have to?'

'I'll get nothing done if you don't!'

'I'll look after him,' said Rex.

Simon came up to him and took his hand.

'Seems to have taken a shine to you,' said Arthur. 'That child's got two great loves – railways and dogs!'

They followed Arthur along the tracks to where an old steam engine sat in a siding. They watched while Arthur fired the boiler, then they helped him build up the blaze.

Simon helped by passing them lumps of coal, occasionally wiping his hands on Rex's white shirt.

Before long the fire was blazing merrily.

Rex looked at a gauge. 'The needle's nearly up to the black line.'

Arthur nodded. 'We're about ready. Who's going to drive?'

'Me, me, me!' Simon shrieked.

'Not you, you're trouble,' said Arthur. 'I'll get a box.' He climbed out of the cab.

Michael was unslinging his camera. 'Did you hear what he said? He said one of us could drive! You go first and I'll take your picture. We'll say it was your childhood dream to be an engine-driver. You look the part, too, all covered in coal!'

Arthur came back with a wooden box. He up-ended the box and put it beside the controls.

'If one of you would like to hop up?'

Rex got on to the box.

'It's all very simple,' said Arthur. 'This is the brake, and this is the regulator . . . .' Rex watched intently as the old man demonstrated the operation of the controls. 'All you have to do now is push the regulator across,' said Arthur. 'Go on, then . . .'

Rex moved the regulator while Michael took his picture.

There was a cloud of steam – and to Rex's astonished delight the engine moved slowly forward.

'Right,' said Arthur. 'Now we can collect the coaches and take you out for a ride!'

'It was an amazing afternoon. Rex and Michael were allowed to take turns at driving the engine. It was quite an experience. Then they helped Arthur to couple on some coaches and a guard's van, in preparation for a proper run. They stood, waiting, beside the engine as Arthur made his final checks, getting the full story on the steam railway and its problems.

'You wouldn't think a line of railway track would be so expensive,' said Michael.

'It's not just the track, it's the land and buildings as well,' said Arthur. 'We need all that to keep the line going.'

'They say there's a supermarket chain after it,' said Nora.

'You really can't raise the money?' Rex asked.

'Not that much,' Arthur replied sadly.

The little train pulled away from the platform, chugged along the track, through a cutting and under a little railway bridge.

Rex and Michael sat in the guard's van, putting the finishing touches to their story.

Rex read it out from Michael's notebook. '"Branch-line Tragedy. Heartbroken members of the Nottingham Steam Society are preparing to blow the whistle for the last time as a brand-new supermarket comes steaming into their station."' He looked up. 'Better than a boring old school outing!'

'It's news!' Michael said proudly.

The little train steamed on its way.

It was break-time at school, and Rex and Michael were studying a mock-up of their edition of the school newspaper. The front-page picture showed Rex driving the train.

'We shouldn't just *report* what's happening to those steam railway people,' Rex said suddenly. 'We should try to help them. We could still start a campaign, raise money, get people interested . . .'

Mrs Jessop came into the room and looked critically

at the newspaper. She noticed the front page picture. 'Hey, when was that taken?'

'We went back to have a look at that station, miss,' said Michael.

'And they let you in? What have you two got that I haven't?'

'We're reporters, miss,' said Michael loftily.

'And just what are we reporting?'

Rex saw his opportunity. 'We were thinking we might actually *do* something. Get people interested in saving the line. There's nothing really wrong with it: it just needs cleaning and painting and tidying up.'

One thing about Mrs Jessop, she was a wow at getting things done. 'That sounds easy enough.' She pointed out of the window at the teeming playground. 'And there's your labour force!'

'How do we get them to help?' asked Rex.

'Just ask for volunteers!'

Children were coming in for the next lesson and Mrs Jessop raised her voice.

'Oi, you lot, we need some volunteers.' She pointed her finger. 'We'll have you, you and you – and you as well. Come to think of it, we'll have the lot of you!'

Next weekend Mrs Jessop's class descended on the little station in force. They brought mops, buckets, brooms and cleaning materials of every kind, all borrowed from bemused parents.

They swept and cleaned and dusted and polished and mopped. They cleared up rubble and rubbish and stowed it away.

They climbed all over the old locomotives, polishing them till they gleamed. They painted and decorated the platform and the waiting room. They put up a big banner saying:

SAVE OUR STATION!

At the end of a weekend's hard work, the station was transformed. Old Arthur and Nora were amazed and delighted – and full of new hope . . .

Mr Thomas was reading the new *Oakwood Times* over supper in the kitchen. 'This looks really great, Michael.'

'Thanks, Mr Thomas,' Michael replied modestly. 'This is only the beginning.'

'We've started our own Save the Branch-line campaign,' said Rex.

Mr Thomas studied the paper. 'I see Mrs Jessop's involved as well. "We have the station, we have the trains, we have the will to win! Now all we need is the public." Did she really say that?'

'More or less,' said Rex. 'She said we needed publicity. We just souped it up a bit!'

'It says here she's organizing a press conference on Saturday.'

'All the journalists are going to come along and be taken for a ride on the train.'

'Then they'll see how brilliant the place is,' said Michael. 'They'll write it up in their papers, everyone will send money and the line will be saved!'

But it wasn't like that. On Saturday morning Mrs Jessop had everything set up in the station booking office. There was a handwritten banner saying SAVE OUR STATION. On a table underneath it, Mrs Jessop and old Arthur sat, waiting to answer questions.

In front of the table were rows of chairs all ready for the journalists.

But all the chairs were empty – well, all but one. The only journalist who'd turned up was Michael.

Mrs Jessop looked at her watch. 'We'll give them another ten minutes, shall we?'

Rex was standing at the ticket barrier with a pile of leaflets to hand to passers-by. Even though the publicity campaign had been a dead loss with journalists, it had managed to attract quite a few passengers for the steam-train ride.

Rex was being 'helped' by Simon. Simon's idea of helping was to try and close the barrier whenever anyone wanted to come in.

Suddenly Rex started to itch.

'Stay here,' he told Simon sternly and dashed into the station. Simon waited for a few minutes, got bored and wandered off . . .

Mrs Jessop stood up. 'Doesn't look as if anyone's going to turn up, Arthur. We'd better call it a day.'

Michael stood up. 'I'm a journalist from the *Oakwood Times*, and I'd like to ask a question. Where do you go from here?'

'We don't,' Mrs Jessop snapped in reply.

'One more question,' said Michael.

'Well?'

'How old are you?'

'Michael,' said Mrs Jessop gently.

'Yes, miss?'

'Go and jump in the lake!'

The train was standing at the platform, with most of

the passengers already on board. Nora was waiting by the engine in a clean set of overalls.

Mrs Jessop and Arthur walked along the platform towards her, while Michael, camera at the ready, headed for the footbridge to cover the departure of the train.

Nora came down the platform to meet them, unaware of a small figure behind her who was climbing into the cab of the engine.

'How did it go?' asked Nora.

'No journalists turned up,' said Mrs Jessop.

'Never mind, we tried,' said Nora. She looked at Arthur. 'Where's Simon? I thought you had him.'

Arthur shook his head. 'I thought he was with you . . .'

He glanced over her shoulder and his eyes widened. 'Who's driving the train?'

'I am,' said Nora. 'But it's not leaving till I find Simon.'

'It's already left!' said Arthur.

They turned and saw that the train was gliding away from the platform.

'Simon!' said Arthur. He dashed for the moving train and just managed to scramble into the guard's van.

At the same moment, Rex, in his dog shape, trotted out of the station. He took one look at the moving train with its empty engine, and he guessed that something had gone wrong.

He scampered up the steps of the footbridge, sprang-up onto the parapet – and took a flying leap on to the roof of the guard's van as it trundled by. He didn't even notice Michael standing there with his camera – but Michael got a magnificent shot of the dog's daring leap.

After landing on top of the guard's van, the dog

trotted forward and leapt on to the roof of the next carriage. It ran the length of the carriage and sprang for the next one, working its way towards the engine.

Arthur ran from the guard's van into the last carriage and opened the window.

'Who's driving the train?' a nervous-looking lady asked.

'I am,' said Arthur.

The lady looked terrified.

Arthur managed to climb half way out of the window. He wanted to get on to the roof, if he could manage it. There was a connecting corridor, and it was the only way to reach the engine.

He pulled himself up so he could see over the edge of the roof – and was amazed to see a little dog scampering over the carriage roofs towards the engine.

Rex reached the front carriage, jumped down to the coal tender, scrambled across the coal and jumped into the cab.

Simon sat, huddled up in the corner, looking very frightened.

It was pretty obvious what had happened: somehow Simon had sneaked into the cab and pushed the regulator, setting the train in motion. And now it was gathering speed!

Fortunately the box was still in place. Rex shoved it along with his two front paws till it was underneath the brake. He jumped up on to the box and pushed the brake-lever down with his paw.

The train began to slow to a halt . . .

Mr Thomas studied the headline in his morning paper.

'WONDER-DOG SAVES TODDLER' it said in big black letters. The accompanying picture showed a dog leaping from a footbridge on to the roof of a moving train.

'Nice publicity!' said Mr Thomas. 'And they used Michael's photo!'

'They paid him a packet for it, too,' said Rex. 'Mrs Jessop "suggested" he gave the money to the Save the Railway fund!'

'What a nice thought,' said Mr Thomas. 'Well, a story like this ought to capture the public interest . . .'

And so it did. Next Saturday, in the station office, Arthur, Nora, Michael and Mrs Jessop watched a group of children struggling with sacks and sacks of mail. There were hundreds and hundreds of letters – and nearly all of them contained cheques, postal orders and cash.

'It's wonderful,' said Arthur. 'We've nearly reached our fund target already! We can buy the station and keep it going!'

'A very satisfactory ending,' said Mrs Jessop.

They all went out on to the platform where the train was standing, ready to leave. It was nearly full, and the last few passengers were climbing aboard.

'We'd never have managed without your help,' said Arthur.

'It was the children really,' said Mrs Jessop. 'And the dog!'

The little dog was trotting up and down the platform like a sheepdog, barking at the stragglers to get them on to the train.

'I think he's trying to tell me something!' said Arthur. He hurried off to the engine and climbed into the cab.

The little dog ran along to the guard's van and jumped inside. Seconds later, he stuck his head out through the open window, a whistle clenched in his jaws. The dog blew a piercing blast, and the train started moving. The dog disappeared.

'How did he learn to do that?' asked Mrs Jessop.

'I think he just likes trains, miss,' said Michael.

Mrs Jessop looked around. 'Where's Rex?'

'Working, miss,' said Michael.

'Poor Rex,' said Mrs Jessop. 'He's missing all the fun!'

The dog reappeared in the guard's van window and Michael took a quick photo.

He waved at the dog, Rex woofed in reply and the train pulled away.

Get Me to
the Church

Rex was running out of time.

He stopped mowing the lawn and looked at his watch, then he looked at the amount of lawn he still had to finish and came to a decision. Five minutes later, he was hurrying round to the front of the house.

His bike was leaning against the garage wall, and the garage door was open. Rex went inside. His teacher, Mrs Jessop, was just emerging from underneath an ancient Morris Minor. It was a very different Mrs Jessop from the smartly dressed terror of class seven. She wore greasy old dungarees and a headscarf, and looked like a heroic factory worker in an old movie.

'Know anything about cars, Rex?'

'Not a lot, miss.'

'It's an awful bore, but I think I'm going to have to have the engine out again. What can I do for you?'

'I'm off now, miss,' Rex said hurriedly. 'I've put the mower away and emptied the grass on the compost heap . . .'

'And the lawn? Am I going to like what I see?'

'It's not *quite* finished, miss.'

Mrs Jessop gave him her beady-eyed look. 'Rex, when we struck our deal, when I rashly paid you a handsome sum for two hours' toil, I foolishly thought that the two hours would be spent in mowing my lawn – not in drinking me out of orange juice and leaving the job half done.'

'I'm really sorry, miss. I'll come back and finish tomorrow.'

'You'd better,' said Mrs Jessop.

Rex looked at his watch. 'It's just that I'm due round at Michael's house. It's his big sister Eileen's wedding.'

'Oh yes,' said Mrs Jessop. 'I'm going myself, I must stop all this and get changed soon.' She smiled. 'As a matter of fact, it was I who brought the happy couple together: I put them both in detention. I remember I told Jason he ought to become a professional cricketer – and now he's a pop star.'

'He's not a pop star yet, miss.'

'If the girls in the class hung on to my every word the way they do to his, we'd be through the history syllabus in six weeks. See you in church, Rex.' She slid back under the car.

Rex got on his bike, then paused for a moment. 'Miss, why did you put Jason in detention?'

'For only mowing half my lawn!'

Rex rode hurriedly away.

A few minutes later he was riding down a quiet back street, and pulling up outside the house of his best mate, Michael Tully. He wheeled his bike through the side entrance, parked it in the yard and knocked on the kitchen door.

Michael appeared, wearing a proper suit with a white carnation in the lapel. Rex grinned. Mike threatened him with his fist and ushered him inside. As Rex came into the kitchen, the sound of smashing china, followed by violent sobbing, came from upstairs.

Michael winced. 'Eileen can't find her lucky troll!' There was the sound of more smashing and more sobs. 'She says it's the happiest day of her life!'

Out in the hall the telephone rang. Michael went to answer it.

'Hello.' He yelled up the stairs, 'Eileen, it's Jason!'

He put the receiver down beside the phone, then turned back into the kitchen. Rex heard the sound of feet running downstairs and caught a glimpse of Michael's big sister Eileen, resplendent in a traditional white wedding dress. She picked up the phone.

Michael came back into the kitchen, closing the door.

'Jason will calm her down, he always does.'

From the hall came the sound of Eileen's angry voice. Suddenly she slammed down the phone, and they heard her footsteps pounding back up the stairs. A door slammed somewhere overhead.

'Nerves!' said Michael. 'She'll be all right when we get to the church!' As he spoke, two little girls in fancy white bridesmaid's dresses ran excitedly into the kitchen. They were Patricia and Imelda, Michael's younger sisters.

'Eileen's not going to the church,' Patricia announced. 'She's locked herself in her room!'

'What?' said Michael.

'We heard her on the phone,' Imelda explained.

Patricia nodded. 'She said, "How can you do this to me, Jason? And at the last minute!"'

'You must have got it wrong,' said Michael.

'We haven't!' Patricia insisted.

Mr Tully, Michael's father, came into the kitchen. Like Michael he was wearing a formal suit and a white carnation. He pulled open a dresser drawer filled with odds and ends and started rooting through it.

Michael gave him a worried look. 'Everything okay, Dad?'

'Just seeing if there's a spare key to Eileen's room.'

'See!' Patricia said triumphantly.

Michael looked at Rex. 'We'd better see what's going on.'

They went upstairs, and found Mrs Tully, all dressed up for the wedding, standing outside Eileen's bedroom door.

'I'm sure he didn't mean it like that, Eileen. Why don't you ring him up and talk it over?'

A muffled sob came from behind the door. 'What's the point? He doesn't want me!'

Mr Tully came charging up the stairs. 'Is this true? He's jilted her?'

'There does seem to be a problem,' Mrs Tully admitted.

'Nobody jilts my little girl,' said Mr Tully. 'I'm going round to see young Jason!' He headed back downstairs.

'Don't do anything you'll be sorry for,' said Mrs Tully. 'I'd better come with you. Michael, you look after the girls, give them some biscuits or something!' She hurried after her husband and the front door slammed behind them.

Michael went down to the kitchen, found the biscuits and gave them to his sisters, and told them to go and sit in their bedroom, stuff themselves and shut up. He rejoined Rex outside the bedroom door. 'Maybe she'll listen to you?' Rex suggested.

Michael went to the door. 'Feeling any better? How about coming out now, we're all ready.'

'Go away!'

'Marriage is a really good thing,' Rex said encouragingly. 'Sets a good example to young people like us!'

'You have a duty to come out and get married,' said Michael sternly. 'Oh, come on, Eileen, please!'

Suddenly Rex started scratching. He gave Michael a helpless look and ran downstairs. Michael stared at the locked door for a moment and then followed him.

He found Rex the dog in the middle of the kitchen floor struggling to get free of a pile of Rex the boy's clothes.

Michael went over to help him, gathering up the clothes and stowing them in a cupboard. He was so used to the change by now that he went on talking to Rex as if nothing had happened.

'There must be something we can do, Rex. I'm sure she'd be fine if someone sensible could just talk to her calmly. Someone she really likes.'

Rex cocked his head and tapped his own chest with his paw.

'Woof!'

'Hey, there's an idea!'

They went back upstairs. Michael waited at the top while Rex went over to Eileen's door. He scratched at it with his paw and began whining pitifully. He waited for a moment, then scratched and whined again.

The door opened a little and Eileen peered out. 'Bobby! What are you doing here?'

Rex wriggled through the gap, and the door closed behind him.

Michael grinned and went back downstairs.

The front door opened and his parents poured in.

'It's not him, it's her!' said Mr Tully. '*She* called off the wedding!'

'Don't worry, it'll all be sorted out soon,' Michael said hopefully. 'I've got someone inside.'

'Who?'

'Bobby the dog. I think he may be able to get round her.'

In the bedroom Eileen was sitting on the floor by the bed. She was hugging Rex so hard he found it hard to breathe. The door-handle rattled and she heard her father's voice.

'Now come on, Eileen, stop this silliness!'

Then her mother: 'Open the door, pet. The car will be round soon.'

'Well, you can send it away,' Eileen called. 'I'm not coming out!'

'I'm warning you, Eileen . . .' said her father's voice sternly.

Eileen ignored it, hugging the little dog even harder.

Outside the door Mr Tully was shouting, 'A lot of people are coming to see you get married and I won't have them let down. Do you want me to break the door down?' Silence. 'All right, stand back, I'm coming in!' Mr Tully hurled himself against the door.

But it wasn't like the cop movies on the telly. He just bounced off again.

Attracted by the noise, Patricia and Imelda came out of their room. 'Dad . . .' said Imelda.

'Not now, Daddy's busy,' said Mrs Tully. She turned to her husband. 'Frank, you'll break the door . . .'

'What do you think I'm trying to do?' her husband snarled. He slammed against the door again and gave a yelp of pain.

'You'll break your shoulder as well if you go on like that,' said Mrs Tully practically.

Rubbing his shoulder, Mr Tully decided to abandon brute force. 'I demand that you open this door!'

Nothing happened.

Mr Tully pounded on the door with his fist, jarring his bruised shoulder. 'Aaargh!' He leaned, panting against the door. 'This is your last chance, Eileen!'

Eileen's voice came from the other side of the door. 'I've got the key here, Dad, and I'm going to throw it out of the window . . .' Her voice came again, a little more distant. 'There! It's gone right over the lane into someone's garden. I'm never coming out!'

'That's it,' Mr Tully shouted. 'I'm ringing the fire brigade!'

'Come on, Frank,' said his wife. 'We can't *make* her get married. We'd better get down to the church and tell the guests.'

'Did you hear that, Eileen?' Mr Tully called. 'Your mother's going to cancel the wedding.'

'Good!'

'All right,' said Mrs Tully wearily. 'Girls, Michael, everybody into the car.'

'Is it time to go to the wedding?' Imelda asked.

Mrs Tully sighed. 'I don't think there's going to be a wedding today!'

In the bedroom Eileen was still hugging the little dog.

'He doesn't care about me, he only cares about his stupid band,' she sobbed. 'Imagine, announcing on your wedding day that you're going to fly home in the middle of the honeymoon because you're playing in a concert with Take That!'

Wriggling free, Rex went over to the dressing table

and jumped up on a stool. Taking a packet of tissues, he jumped down and carried them to Eileen.

Eileen blew her nose and wiped her eyes. 'Thanks . . . He says it's his big break . . . I said "What about me, I've been waiting for this honeymoon for years, don't I get a break?"'

Rex went over to the bed and took down a fluffy rabbit, depositing it in front of Eileen. Then he pulled down a teddy bear, a giraffe, a hippo and a kangaroo, arranging them in a row.

'I know what you're trying to do, dog,' she sniffed. 'You're trying to make me think he's a wonderful person, just because he bought me all these. Well, it won't work!'

Rex added a giant pink poodle to the collection.

Eileen sniffed. 'He gave me that when I passed my GCEs. So he should have, I got very good grades . . .'

Rex went to the dressing table and picked up a framed photograph of Jason. Holding it carefully in his jaws, he carried it over to Eileen.

She took the photograph and looked at it. 'Just because he gives me presents, and takes me places and is nice to me . . .' She burst into tears.

The little dog disappeared under the bed, scrabbled around for a while, then came back with something in his mouth. He put the something into Eileen's hands. It was an ugly little doll.

'My lucky troll!' Eileen shrieked. 'It's a sign! I've got to get to the church, I can't let him down!' She rushed to the mirror. 'I look awful! Still, brides always cry, don't they?'

'Woof! Woof!'Rex said encouragingly. Putting his front paws on the dressing table, he passed her a hairbrush.

While Eileen brushed her hair, Rex went to the wardrobe and fetched her white shoes. He went over to a florist's box, tipped open the lid with his paw and picked up the bouquet, carrying it to Eileen.

She stood up, holding the bouquet. 'Do I look all right?'

'Woof!'

'You say the nicest things, pity you're not a boy!' Eileen looked around. 'Flowers, veil, Jason's got my passport ...' She went to the door and turned the handle. It was locked. She looked towards the open window, remembering what she'd done with the key. 'Oh no!'

The little dog jumped up on the window-sill and took a flying leap out of the window. Eileen ran to look and saw it perched on the garden wall. It walked along the wall and woofed encouragingly. It went back to the point where the wall met the house and tapped a drainpipe with its paw.

'You're kidding!'

'Woof!'

Eileen sat on the window-sill and looked down. The drainpipe ran down the side of the house, and then horizontally across. The end of the drainpipe was very close to the top of the wall.

'You think I can climb along that thing?'

'Woof!'

Eileen shook her head. 'I'm sitting on a window-sill in my wedding dress, arguing with a dog!'

She took a deep breath, put her wedding bouquet between her teeth and lowered herself out of the window.

A little boy, walking along the lane between the houses, looked up and saw a girl in a bridal dress hanging out of a window. Interested, he stopped to watch.

Eileen lowered herself until her feet were touching the horizontal angle of the drainpipe. Holding the window-ledge, she edged her way along as far as she could. When she could go no further, she reached out with one hand and gripped the window-sill of the next room, transferring her grip to that. She moved to the end of the next sill, took one foot off the drainpipe and found the top of the wall. She stretched out her other foot and let go of the pipe. She was standing on top of the wall, swaying precariously.

There was a round of applause. Eileen looked down and saw that an appreciative little crowd had gathered in the lane.

Rex ran along the top of the wall to join her.

'You were right,' said Eileen. 'I didn't kill myself!'

She walked carefully along the wall and jumped down into her own backyard. She ran to the back door. It was locked. She ran back into the lane.

'They've all gone to a wedding,' said the little boy helpfully. 'I saw them set off in the car.'

Eileen heard a sudden 'Woof!' She turned and saw the little dog standing beside Rex's green mountain bike in the yard, its front paws on the saddle.

'Oh no!' said Eileen.

'Woof!'

A few minutes later she was wobbling along the lane, Rex trotting beside her.

They rode out of the lane, along a side road and into the high street. People stared, pointed and laughed. Eileen gritted her teeth and pedalled on. Suddenly she noticed the little dog had disappeared.

Then she heard a loud 'Woof!' just ahead and saw the dog standing by the entrance to a minicab office.

Eileen steered the bike to the kerb and jumped off. Propping the bike up on the kerb, she dashed into the office, Rex at her heels.

A bored-looking girl was sitting behind the little counter filing her nails.

'We need a car please,' Eileen gasped. 'St Mary's Church, Grove Road.'

'Certainly, miss. When would that be for?'

'Now, please. I'm getting married in twenty minutes!'

'Ah! Can I interest you in our white limousine service?'

'Anything! I just need to get to the church.'

The girl studied a wall-chart. 'Unfortunately, all our limousines are booked for the day. In fact, *all* our cars are out at the present moment.'

'You've got no cars free at all?'

'That seems to be the situation as of at present.'

Eileen turned and dashed out of the office, Rex close behind. She ran to the kerb. The mountain bike was gone! The dog peered up and down the street, growling fiercely.

'Oh no!' said Eileen. 'What am I going to tell Rex?' She heard a volley of barks and saw that the little dog was trotting along the pavement towards an approaching policeman.

'Must keep going!' Eileen muttered. She ran up to the policeman. 'I'm trying to get to my wedding and my bike's been stolen!'

'Your bike, miss?'

Eileen was on the verge of tears. 'It's not even my

bike really, I only borrowed it. I don't know what I'm going to do . . .'

Constable Norman was moved by the sight of a damsel in distress. 'Why don't you come down to the station with me?'

'But I've got to be at the church in ten minutes!'

'Maybe we can help you. Our station inspector is dead keen on good community relations . . .'

A few minutes later, Eileen was being ushered into a police car by a friendly young policewoman called Fleming, while PC Norman held the door.

'What about the little dog?' he asked.

'He's got to come too,' said Eileen. 'It was all his idea!'

Rex jumped in the back beside Eileen. PC Norman closed the door, went round to the front of the car and got behind the wheel. WPC Fleming got in beside him. The police car drove away.

'This is very kind of you,' said Eileen.

'Can't have you missing your wedding, can we?' said PC Norman. 'St Mary's, is it?'

'Woof!' said Rex.

'Bright little chap, isn't he?' said WPC Fleming.

Suddenly they came to a 'Road Closed' sign blocking the way. A 'Diversion' sign pointed down a side road.

'Roadworks,' PC Norman explained. 'Have to make a bit of a detour, past the park.'

Rex started barking furiously.

WPC Fleming turned around. 'I'm sorry, but we've got to. It's the law!'

But Rex was barking at something through the window. Eileen looked out. 'That's our bike!' she shouted. 'The green one!'

A skinhead was pedalling Rex's mountain bike down the road.'

'Bernie Lampton!' said WPC Fleming.

'It would be,' said PC Norman. He overtook the cyclist and screeched to a halt in front of him. At the sight of the police car, the skinhead jumped off the bike, dashed into the park and disappeared into the distance. The two police officers scrambled out of the car and ran after him.

Eileen looked at the little dog. 'Now what?'

Rex jumped over the back seat and out through the open front door of the car. He ran to his abandoned bike. 'Woof!'

Eileen got out of the car and walked over to him. 'We take off? Just like that?'

'Woof!'

'You're right! You're always right!'

She got on the bike and began following the route indicated by the diversion sign.

Rex jumped up and down in front of her. 'Woof!'

Eileen stopped and looked back. 'We can take a short cut through here? You sure?'

'Woof!'

Rex led her through a hedge and up a track that led to a disused railway embankment. They crossed the embankment, sailed down another track and rejoined the road. As they passed a little side road, Eileen saw a phone box at the far corner. It was a one-way street, so Eileen jumped off the bike and pushed it towards the phone box. Rex saw that she wasn't following, ran back and stood in front of her, head cocked inquiringly.

'If I could just get the vicar's number,' Eileen explained, 'I'm sure his housekeeper would pop round to the church and tell him I'm on the way.'

Rex moved aside, and Eileen pushed the bike up to the phone box and propped it against the kerb. They both went into the phone box.

In the Tullys' car, tempers were getting frayed.

'I am not lost!' Mr Tully insisted. 'I just missed my bearings somewhere round that roadworks diversion.'

'We've already been down this road,' said Mrs Tully. 'Twice!'

'All right, all right!' Mr Tully snapped. 'We'll try down there.' He turned into a side street with a phone box at the end.

'No!' shouted Michael, but it was too late.

An approaching car shot towards them, blaring its horn. Mr Tully swerved to avoid it.

'Idiot!' he shouted.

'It's a one-way street,' Michael yelled. 'And we're going the wrong way!'

Another car whizzed by, blasting at them with its horn. Behind it was a police car.

'Stop the car!' Mrs Tully demanded.

Mr Tully stopped. The police car drove up to them and stopped.

A young policeman put his head out of the window.

'And where are you going, sir?'

'I'm trying to get to my daughter's wedding.'

PC Norman frowned. 'She's not travelling by bicycle by any chance?'

'She's not travelling at all,' said Mr Tully wildly. 'She's not even getting married. I'm going to the church to tell the guests it's all off!'

'Not the wrong way down a one-way street, you're not. Turn round and go back the way you came.'

As Mr Tully opened his mouth to protest, Mrs Tully said, 'Just do it, Frank! Thank you, officer.'

The police car drove on. Furiously Mr Tully flung the car into a sprawling three-point turn. As he swung round by the phone box, he knocked over Rex's bike and ran over it. By now he was so worked up that he didn't even notice.

Imelda peered out of the back window. 'Dad!'

Mr Tully drove on.

'Dad, I saw Eileen, she was in a phone box!'

'Quiet, will you?' Mr Tully snapped.

He was just about to pull out of the side street on to the main road.

'Dad, you hit something!' said Patricia.

The distraction was fatal. Mr Tully tried to go forward and look back at the same time – and ran into an approaching taxi. Both vehicles skidded to a halt.

'What? What did I hit?'

'You hit a taxi, Dad,' said Michael helpfully.

Eileen stood, looking at the flattened bike.

'That's it,' said Eileen wearily. 'I'm just not meant to get there! Now Rex will really kill me!'

She heard a frantic barking and saw the little dog standing at the end of the side road beside the telephone boxes. Rex barked again. Dazedly, Eileen followed him.

The little dog led her along the road, crossed another road and then stopped outside a familiar house with a half-mowed lawn. Rex ran up to the front door, jumped onto a plant pot and rang the front-door bell with his paw.

The door opened at once, revealing Mrs Jessop in

all her wedding finery. 'Eileen? What are you doing here? I thought you were my taxi.'

'Trying to get to the church, miss,' said Eileen.

'Well, I'm very glad to see you, at least I know I haven't missed the wedding. My taxi's late.'

'Could you give me a lift, please, miss?'

The phone in the hall rang and Mrs Jessop turned to answer it. She listened for a moment and then said, 'Then send another! *How* long . . .? I'll have to, won't I?' Slamming down the phone she said, 'Would you believe it? My taxi's been in an accident, and they don't know when they can send me another one! And my car's laid up as well!'

Rex ran to the garage and began barking loudly.

'What does he want in there?' Mrs Jessop asked.

'I don't know, miss, but it usually pays to do what he says!'

They went over to the garage and Rex led them inside. He ran to the back of the garage and woofed loudly.

'That old thing!' said Mrs Jessop. 'Well, it's an idea . . .'

At the scene of the car crash, things were in a state of chaos. An enraged taxi-driver had Mr Tully bent backwards over the bonnet of his car, and was doing his best to throttle him. Michael and Mrs Tully were trying to haul the taxi-driver off.

A police car drew up, a policeman and policewoman got out, and the combatants were separated.

PC Norman looked at Mr Tully. 'It's not really your day today, is it, sir?'

'He crashed into me,' spluttered Mr Tully. 'Now my car won't go and I've got to get to —'

'I know,' said PC Norman. 'Your daughter's wedding. I think there's only one way to deal with this . . .'

Inside St Mary's Church, the bridegroom and the guests were sitting, waiting patiently. Outside the church, the vicar and the photographers were standing waiting, looking anxiously up the road. The vicar looked at his watch. Suddenly a couple of police cars drove up and the Tully family piled out. At the same moment a photographer yelled, 'Here comes the bride!'

A tandem was making its stately way towards them, Mrs Jessop at the back, Eileen at the front, and a little dog in the basket. They dismounted and Mrs Jessop straightened the bride's veil.

'My bouquet!' said Eileen. 'I lost it on the way!'

The dog jumped out of the basket, rushed into the church porch, took a bunch of flowers from a vase and carried them back to Eileen. She took them and patted his head.

Mr Tully gave Eileen a kiss, and they headed for the church, the rest of the family following.

Michael bent down to Rex and whispered, 'I can't wait to hear how you did it!'

'Woof!' said Rex.

Waiting at the altar, Jason turned to see his bride-to-be coming down the aisle on her father's arm, a bit bedraggled but still radiant.

Behind them trotted a scruffy little dog, proudly carrying the bride's train in its mouth!

Goodbye Mrs Chips

It was Friday afternoon and it was games period. Class seven were having cricket practice at the nets. Mrs Jessop was in charge.

'Eye on the ball, Edward, eye on the ball!' she bellowed, as a fast one whizzed straight past the unfortunate boy who was batting.

A small boy dashed across the sports field and stood panting in front of Mrs Jessop. 'Miss, miss!'

'What is it, Denzil?'

'Miss, Mr Farthington wants everyone in the hall for extra choir practice, miss.'

Mr Farthington was the new music teacher. Sharp-faced and sharp-tongued, he had managed to make himself amazingly unpopular with everyone – especially with Mrs Jessop.

She frowned down at Denzil. 'Now?'

'Yes, miss.'

'Well, you can tell Mr Farthington we'll be along as soon as we've finished here – in about half an hour. Got that?'

'Yes, miss.'

Denzil fled, and Mrs Jessop returned to her coaching.

'Where was I? Oh yes. Eye on the ball, Edward.'

She marched up to him and took the bat, demon-
strating the stroke.

'Elbow right up. Watch it all the way on to the
bat and then follow through. Now, let's see you do
it.'

She handed him the bat, and the practice went on.
Rex and Michael were among the group of watchers
waiting for their turn.

'I bet old Farthington did mean now,' Michael
whispered.

Rex nodded. 'He does it to upset her – he could
have organized extra choir practice any time.'

Suddenly they saw a tall figure striding across the
sports field and marching up to Mrs Jessop. 'Did you
get my message?'

'Ah, Mr Farthington! Denzil had some cockeyed
message about you wanting everyone in the hall.'

'That is correct.'

'Now?'

'Now, Mrs Jessop. There's only a week to Open
Day, so extra choir practice is very important.' He
raised his voice. 'Come on, everyone, back to the hall.
Mrs Jessop will tidy up. We don't want to waste any
more time!'

The children hesitated, looking at Mrs Jessop. She
nodded, and they all scurried away. Grim-faced, she
began picking up cricket pads and stumps.

In the hall the choir was arranged on three levels. Rex
and Michael were in the back row, standing on a
rostrum. They were singing 'Old MacDonald Had A
Farm' and chatting behind their song-sheets at the
same time.

'She didn't like it, did she?' Rex whispered. 'Did

you see her face?' Seeing Mr Farthington's eye on him, he added a rapid, '*Ee-i-ee-i-oh!*'

'I know,' said Michael.' But she couldn't say anything, not with all of us there.'

'He's got a nerve,' Michael grumbled. 'He's only been here three weeks.' He joined the chorus: '*Old MacDonald had a farm . . .*'

Suddenly Rex started scratching. He slipped down off the back of the rostrum, and Michael moved along to cover the gap.

Mr Farthington rapped the rostrum with his baton.

'Eyes on me at the back there! We'll take it from "... had a dog". Let's have some attack and enthusiasm, please!'

He flourished the baton and the choir started singing.

'*On that farm he had a dog . . .*

'*Oww-oww-oww-oww oww!*'

A terrible, doggy howling came from behind the rostrum.

'We don't need any extra animal sound-effects, thank you,' said Mr Farthington sharply. 'Now, try again – and concentrate.'

Michael slid down the back of the rostrum and crouched beside the shaggy little dog. 'Rex, I know you can't help it – but try!'

The choir sang again. '*On that farm he had a dog . . .*'

Now he was a dog, Rex just couldn't stop himself. He raised his nose to the skies and joined in. '*Oww-oww-oww-oww oww!*'

'So we have a comedian, do we?' Mr Farthington thundered. He saw the gap in the back row. 'What is going on back there?'

Michael scrambled back on to the rostrum. 'I fell off, sir.'

'So I see!'

Mr Farthington moved to go round to the back of the choir.

'It might have been me who made that strange noise, sir. I've got a bit of a frog in my throat.'

'Sure it wasn't a *dog* in your throat?' said Mr Farthington.

Everyone laughed, the way they always do at teachers' jokes.

'Sorry, sir,' said Michael, when the laughter died down.

'You will close your mouth, Tully,' said Mr Farthington. 'You will not open it again until I tell you. Clear?'

'Yes, sir.'

'I said shut, Tully!'

Mr Farthington returned to his music-stand. 'Let's take it from the top – with no more animal noises, please!'

'Please, Rex, block your ears,' hissed Michael over his shoulder. But it was no use.

'*Old MacDonald had a farm*,' sang the choir.

Behind them rose Rex's high-pitched doggy howl.

'*Oww-oww-oww-oww oww!*'

Mr Farthington stopped the choir. 'Right, that's it, Tully! Go to your classroom and write out five hundred times "I must not be a total idiot during choir practice".'

Michael got down off the rostrum and walked out of the hall.

Rex the dog crawled under the rostrum, dragging his clothes with him, and looked for a way out. The hall's back door was just opposite. Rex pushed the door open with his nose and disappeared down the corridor.

*

Michael was sitting in an empty classroom writing out his lines when he heard a scratching at the door. He got up and opened it. Rex trotted into the room.

'I thought you'd be home by now.'

'Woof!'

'Well, you'd better get a move on, old Farthington will be back soon.'

'Woof! Woof!'

'Of course, the main doors will be shut. Come on then, I'll let you out.'

Michael led Rex out of the classroom. They were hurrying down the long corridor when a door opened at the far end and they saw Mrs Jessop coming towards them.

Instinctively they turned and retraced their steps.

They hadn't got very far when, somewhere ahead of them, they heard a voice raised in anger. It was Mr Farthington.

'So we all want to be animal impressionists, do we?'

Michael ducked back into the classroom, and Rex tried to follow. 'Not in here!' Michael hissed. 'He's bound to come in!'

Rex darted into an empty classroom opposite.

A moment later Mr Farthington appeared, dragging Denzil by the ear.

'I don't care if they are threatened with extinction,' he was saying. 'Old MacDonald did *not* have a spider monkey!'

He thrust the boy towards the door of Michael's classroom.

'Tully will show you what to do!'

Mr Farthington turned − and found himself facing Mrs Jessop.

'I'd like a word, please,' she snapped.

'Could we make it after I've finished choir practice?'

'Finish it now,' said Mrs Jessop in a tone that had icicles on it. 'I'll be in here.' She went into the class-room opposite – the same one Rex had hidden in.

Luckily there were some cardboard boxes stacked in a corner, and Rex just had time to wriggle behind them. He heard Mrs Jessop pacing up and down for a few minutes, then someone else came into the room.

'Can we make this quick?' said Mr Farthington. 'I have left thirty children tidying up the hall – which probably means reducing it to matchwood.'

Mrs Jessop got straight to the point. 'I cannot have my cricket practice interrupted.'

Mr Farthington sighed. 'You've brought me in here for this?'

'Your behaviour was totally unprofessional.'

'On the contrary,' said Mr Farthington loftily. 'When the parents and governors hear my choir on Open Day, they'll realize the degree of amateurishness they've had to put up with in this school until now. I am under consideration for the post of Vice Principal. Nothing, *nothing*, is going to stand in my way!'

'I'm not interested in your career plans,' Mrs Jessop snapped. 'Just don't interrupt my cricket practice again!'

'I can't promise –'

'Try!' said Mrs Jessop.

Mr Farthington drew himself up. 'I am not prepared to let myself down with an under-rehearsed "Runaway Train".'

'And I'm not prepared to see a team of kids who've worked flat out for months lose the Cricket Cup for lack of practice!'

'But that's only games,' said Mr Farthington wearily. 'It's not *important* . . .'

'*I beg your pardon?*' Mrs Jessop replied menacingly.

'Then she hit him with a map-container,' said Rex. 'She was really furious!'

By now Rex had recovered his clothes and returned to his human form. He and Michael were on their way home from school.

'The cricket team's very important to her,' said Michael. 'And to have that idiot Farthington messing her about . . .'

'He even said he was going to be Vice Principal.'

'Above Mrs Jessop? They wouldn't dare.'

'He seemed pretty confident.'

'That would be *awful*!' said Michael. 'We'd have him being horrible – and her in a foul mood as well . . .'

Rex discussed his worries with his father later that evening. 'It wouldn't surprise me if she was thinking about leaving.'

'Mrs Jessop?' said his father. 'She's very happy at the school.'

'She's not, Dad, honestly. I know she's not. It's this new music teacher, Mr Farthington. He's trying to take over the school, I know he is.'

'How do you know?'

'Well . . .' said Rex. The doorbell rang and he jumped up. 'I'll see who it is, shall I?'

'I'll go,' said Mr Thomas, looking at his watch. 'Time you were in your pyjamas. You can watch a bit of telly before bed.'

Rex opened his mouth to argue – and suddenly felt itchy. Scratching furiously, he hurried from the room.

*

Back in his dog shape, Rex sat on top of his pyjamas on the sofa, watching television. The remote control lay on the sofa beside him, and from time to time he reached out and changed channels with his paw.

He watched a bit of a soap opera, a documentary about Chinese art, part of an old thriller he'd already seen three times, and finally some snooker. Yawning, he switched the set to standby, then jumped off the sofa and pushed the off button with his nose.

Grabbing his pyjamas in his teeth, he dragged them over to the door. He climbed on a chair and pushed up the light switch with his nose, then jumped down and carried his pyjamas into the lighted hallway.

As he trotted along the landing towards his bedroom, he heard voices from the kitchen.

'I'm afraid we may have to cancel our cricket coaching arrangement,' Mrs Jessop was saying. 'I'm thinking of resigning.'

Hurriedly dragging his pyjamas into his room, Rex came out on to the landing and slipped quietly into the kitchen.

His father and Mrs Jessop were sitting at the kitchen table, chatting over cups of tea. Rex stretched out under the table, pretending to be asleep.

'Rex told me you weren't getting on too well with this Mr Farthington,' said Mr Thomas. 'Amazing what kids pick up.' He took a swig of his tea. 'One of the school governors, John Wellesby, comes in the shop to buy golf balls. He seems like a very nice man. You could have a word with him . . .'

Mrs Jessop shook her head. 'No, I refuse to beg! If they can't see what's going on, I don't think I want to be part of the school any more.'

*

Early next morning, Rex and Michael were sitting on adjoining swings in the empty park playground, discussing the Mrs Jessop crisis.

'That's terrible,' said Michael. 'We can't let her leave.'

'She sounded pretty determined. Dad suggested she spoke to one of the school governors, but she said she wasn't going to beg.'

Michael nodded. 'She wouldn't, would she. Not her style. We could, though.'

'We could what?'

'Beg,' said Michael. 'We could talk to this governor guy.'

'What would we say?'

Michael thought hard. 'We could say we'd resign if Mrs Jessop goes. Or we could threaten to go on hunger strike!'

'Maybe we'd better just say we want her to stay,' said Rex.

They got off the swings and began walking through the park. Rex was still brooding over the Jessop problem.

'We can't just walk up to this governor and say, "We think Mr Farthington is a pig, please stop Mrs Jessop from leaving." Not just like that. We'd have to pick the right moment.'

'How do we do that?'

'I don't know,' said Rex thoughtfully. 'We need to get him in our debt somehow.'

'We could return his missing cat?' suggested Michael.

'Suppose it's not missing?'

'We kidnap it first, obviously.'

Rex gave him a look. 'I think we need to check this governor out. I'll find out if Dad knows his address . . .'

*

Early that afternoon, Michael was lying on his stomach in a clump of bushes, surveying a large detached house surrounded by lawns and gardens. In his hand was a walkie-talkie. He'd been given a pair for a recent birthday and he'd insisted on bringing them along, convinced they'd come in useful.

He spoke into the receiver. 'This is definitely the place.'

Rex was standing by two parked bikes on a corner of the road, close to the house. He spoke into his receiver. 'Michael, could we stop using these things and just talk?'

A voice crackled from the handset. 'Okay!'

A few minutes later Michael appeared.

'We could just go over and ring the bell,' he suggested.

Rex shook his head. 'People don't like you just turning up on their doorsteps. We need to bump into him somehow.'

Michael was looking at the house. 'Is that him now?

A distinguished-looking man was coming out of the house. He wore casual clothes and was carrying a golf bag over his shoulder. He opened the back of a red hatchback that was parked in the drive.

'Must be,' said Rex. 'Dad said he was a golfer.'

'The golf course could be a good place to talk to him,' said Michael. 'If he does well, he'll be putty in our hands. My Uncle Jack will do anything for me after a good game of golf.'

'Suppose he has a bad one?'

'He smashes the furniture.'

'We'll have to make sure Mr Wellesby has a good game!'

The car came down the drive and pulled out on to

the road. Rex and Michael jumped on their bikes and followed.

Luckily the golf club was well signposted and not very far away, so they weren't too far behind their quarry when they reached the gates.

There was a little car park close to the club house, and this gave them a bit of cover. Propping up their bikes in the corner, they were just in time to see Mr Wellesby walk out of the car park and head for the club house.

'We could offer to be caddies,' said Rex. 'Carry his golf bag around for him.'

'And when he's done a couple of brilliant shots and is feeling wonderful . . .'

'We bring up the subject of school and Mrs Jessop and say – Oh no! I don't believe it!'

'Why would we say that?'

'I'm saying it now!' Rex had started to scratch.

Mike gave him a worried look. 'Dogs aren't allowed on golf courses, are they?'

'What do I do then?'

'Hide – in those trees over there!'

'Okay.' Rex ducked down behind a car.

'Actually, this could turn out to be useful,' said Michael. 'If he hits his ball into the long grass, you could put it back in the open for him. We need him in a good mood, remember!'

'Woof!' said the little dog from behind the car.

Michael scooped up Rex's clothes and stuffed them into his saddle-bag. He picked up the walkie-talkie.

'Hold on to this, we may need it!'

Rex took the walkie-talkie in his mouth.

'Can you manage?' asked Michael.

The dog looked at him.

'Don't try to answer with your mouth full! I'll go and make contact with Mr Wellesby. Off you go then, and try not to let anyone see you!'

Rex streaked off towards the trees and Michael ran towards the club house, catching up with Mr Wellesby.

'Excuse me, sir!' he called. 'Could I caddy for you?'

'Job Week for the scouts, is it?'

'No, sir, I just want to learn how to play the game. If you let me watch, I'll carry your clubs.'

'That's very kind of you. What's your name?'

'Michael Tully, sir.'

'Well, Michael, if you'd like to get them from the car . . . They're in the red hatchback over there.'

Suddenly a familiar voice called, 'John! There you are.'

Mr Farthington was crossing the car park towards them.

Michael turned and ran.

Mr Wellesby strode over to meet Mr Farthington. 'Perfect timing! I've got a lad who wants to caddy for us. He's just –' He looked around, realizing that Michael was nowhere in sight. Mr Wellesby raised his voice. 'Michael? Michael Tully! Goodness me, he seems to have disappeared!'

Mr Farthington sniffed. 'Doesn't surprise me. He's one of our lot, Mrs Jessop's class. Born troublemaker. You don't want to believe a word he says . . .'

Michael had joined Rex in the wooded part of the golf course.

'I can't talk to Mr Wellesby now, not with old Farthington there. I'll have to try later. I'll go and watch them start, see who's playing when, so you know who to help.' He tapped the walkie-talkie. 'We'll keep in touch with these, okay?'

'Woof!'

Mr Wellesby and Mr Farthington were on the first tee. Michael crouched behind some bushes, whispering into his walkie-talkie. 'Our man's going now . . .'

He watched Mr Wellesby drive off.

'Didn't look too straight to me – see what you can do.'

In the little wood Rex stood listening to the walkie-talkie.

He pressed the button with his paw and said, 'Woof!'

A golf ball came bouncing among the trees and Rex bounded after it. Picking it up in his mouth, he dashed on to the fairway, dropped the ball, and ran back into the woods.

A few minutes later, Mr Wellesby and Mr Farthington appeared, walking up to where the ball was lying.

'Much better than I thought,' said Mr Wellesby. 'I was afraid it was heading into the trees.'

Selecting a club, he prepared to play his next shot.

Mr Wellesby and Mr Farthington finished the first hole and moved on to the next tee. Mr Wellesby was in a cheerful mood.

'It's always nice when you play better than you realize. I was sure that ball had gone into the rough, and it turned out to be in a very good lie. Just shows, doesn't it?'

Michael whispered up from behind a hedge. 'It worked. He really thinks he's playing brilliantly. Can you do any more like that?'

A faint 'Woof!' came from the walkie-talkie.

In a clump of trees close to the second hole, Rex switched off the walkie-talkie with his paw and prepared to go into action. He ran out on to the fairway and saw two balls lying a little way from the green. He dashed up, chose one of them and carried it right on to the green. Then he turned and headed back into cover.

Abandoning the walkie-talkie, which he felt was only a distraction, Rex kept well ahead of the two golfers for the whole of the round. His tactic was to be waiting near each hole as the balls rolled close to the green. While the golfers were still in the distance, Rex adjusted the results. He carried one ball on to the green – and dropped the other back in the rough.

One ball he dug out of a sand bunker and carried to the very edge of the green.

When a ball splashed into the water, Rex dived in and retrieved it. Pausing only to shake himself, the little dog carried the dripping golf ball on to the green.

At each hole he carried one of the two balls close to the flag, so that only a simple putt was needed to hole out.

Occasionally, on the shorter holes, he nosed the ball right into the hole, creating what appeared to be a hole-in-one . . .

It was the most extraordinary game Mr Wellesby had ever taken part in – but he didn't look too happy as Mr Farthington sank his final putt.

'Well, thanks very much John,' Mr Farthington said cheerfully. 'Excellent game!'

Mr Wellesby put the flag-pole back in the hole. 'Certainly was − for you! Not often you see someone get *three* holes-in-one.'

Mr Farthington smiled modestly. 'Funny how one sometimes hits form. Something to tell my grand-children, eh?'

Close by, behind the groundsman's hut, Michael was glaring down at a small shaggy dog.

'What did you do that for? You've totally blown it! *You've been moving the wrong ball!*'

The dog cocked its head. 'Woof?'

'I told you which one to move!'

'Woof! Woof!'

'Yes I did! At least, I tried to. What's the point of having a walkie-talkie if you never answer it?'

A groundsman passing by with his lawnmower stopped to listen.

Michael looked up.

'Do you mind? This is a private conversation!'

Looking rather confused, the groundsman moved on.

Michael turned back to Rex.

'Thanks to you, Farthington's triumphed, Welles-by's going to kick the next kid he sees and Mrs Jessop's certain to leave!'

Looking a picture of canine misery, the little dog sank to the ground in a heap and covered its eyes with its paws.

Immediately Michael felt he'd gone too far.

'Sorry, Rex, it's not all your fault. You did your best. We shouldn't have been cheating anyway.'

All at once Rex sat up and cocked his head thought-fully. Then he jumped up and raced off, disappearing round the corner of the hut. Rex followed and was astonished to see the little dog dashing towards Mr Wellesby and Mr Farthington, who were still chatting close to the eighteenth hole.

'Drinks are on me,' Mr Farthington was saying. 'This calls for champagne, I think!'

The little dog ran up and started gambolling round him.

Mr Wellesby frowned. 'What's a dog doing on the course?'

Mr Farthington shrugged. 'I've really no idea . . .'

He bent down to put his ball in the special pocket in his golf bag. Suddenly the little dog snatched the golf ball from his hand, trotted over to the green with it and dropped it close to the hole. He trotted back and sat at Mr Farthington's feet, looking up at him adoringly.

'Is this your dog, Farthington?' Mr Wellesby asked.

'Certainly not. I've never seen it before.'

The dog scampered back on to the green, picked up the ball, dropped it right in the hole this time, and ran back to Mr Farthington, leaning its head lovingly against his legs.

'You're sure this isn't your dog?' Mr Wellesby asked again.

Mr Farthington shoved the dog away. 'I tell you I have never seen it before. It is not my dog!'

By now a group of golfers was gathering around.

The little dog looked up at Mr Farthington, whining for attention.

'I think he wants you to pat him,' said Mr Wellesby in a dangerously calm voice. 'Reward him for all his good work. He seems to have looked after you very well.'

'Are you saying I've been cheating?'

'I am saying that I don't know how any school can employ a man of your low moral character. It's a matter I shall be taking up with my fellow-governors.'

'Do you really think I'd be stupid enough to train a dog to cheat for me?'

'I should say it was rather clever, teaching it to pick up the right ball and drop it in the hole like that.' Mr Wellesby picked up his golf bag. 'It's all been very instructive. If you don't mind, however, I think I'll give the champagne a miss. Oh, and I should get your dog off the course if I were you.'

He strode away towards the car park.

Watching the scene from behind the hut, Michael suddenly realized that the little dog was nowhere to be seen.

A voice behind him said, 'Michael?'

He turned and saw Rex, back in human shape, standing in the doorway of the groundsman's hut. He was dressed in a black plastic bag with 'Litter' written on it.

'At first I thought you'd gone mad,' said Michael. 'But you were brilliant!'

'Thanks,' said Rex. 'Could you get me my clothes, please?'

The Cricket Cup match was in progress and the school team was heading for a decisive lead.

'Well played,' Mrs Jessop called as a ball soared towards the boundary.

'They're doing well,' said Mr Thomas proudly.

'It's all sort of come together, hasn't it? Thanks for all the coaching.'

'I hear Mr Farthington's moved on,' Mr Thomas said casually. 'It was very sudden, wasn't it?'

'Yes, it was a bit.'

'Any idea why?'

'None,' said Mrs Jessop. 'Just vanished into the night without a trace. No note, nothing!'

'Does that mean you'll be staying on?'

'Oh yes, I think so.' She gave him a dazzling smile. 'They've made me Vice Principal!'

Rex and Michael started to wander off.

'Nice work, Rex,' said Michael.

'It was your idea!'

'Yes, but *I* couldn't have carried a ball in my mouth so well! Lucky you turned into a dog when you did. Don't know how we'd have managed if you hadn't.' He looked thoughtfully at Rex. 'You're not by any chance starting to control it?'

'No, I don't think so,' said Rex. He started scratching, and made a dash for the pavilion.

It was some time later, and Michael was walking away from the cricket field, a shaggy little dog trotting beside him.

'We'll have to work on that,' he said. 'Controlling it, I mean.'

'Woof!' said Rex.

Mr Wonderful

Staggering under the weight of two huge cardboard boxes, Rex and Michael followed Mrs Jessop into the foyer of the hotel.

Mrs Jessop asked directions at reception, and they followed her down a thickly carpeted corridor which ended in a pair of double doors, now standing open. A banner across the doorway read:

MIDLANDS SCHOOLS TECHNOLOGY
FAIR

Inside the long room were rows and rows of tables, with children and teachers busily setting up their exhibits.

One of the organizers was sitting at a card table by the door. Mrs Jessop went up to her. 'Oakwood Middle School.'

The organizer checked a chart. 'Table A 15. Down at the far end by the window.'

'Thank you.' Mrs Jessop turned to the two boys. 'If you'd like to start setting up, I'll organize some refreshments.'

Rex and Michael went over to their table and got to work. At the back of the table they fixed up a screen bearing a number of complicated-looking charts and diagrams. On the table itself they assembled two sizeable wooden boxes. Each box had dials and lights and a small speaker that was set into the lid.

Rex strapped something that looked like a futuristic watch on his wrist, lifted the lid of one of the boxes and moved his hand around over the complex wiring system inside.

The box made a faint buzzing noise.

'Should be louder than that,' Rex muttered. He took an ammeter from his tool-box and started poking about inside.

'Can you fix it?'

'Oh yes, plenty of time to test it before the judging. Pass me the pliers, would you?'

Michael rummaged inside the tool-box. 'They're not here.'

'What?'

'The pliers. We must have left them at school. I'll see if I can borrow some.'

Michael went out of the room and down the corridor into the busy hotel foyer. Lots of people were standing around expectantly, as if something important was about to happen. Quite a few of them were carrying professional-looking cameras.

He made his way over to the hall porter. 'Excuse me, I was wondering if I could borrow a pair of pliers, please.'

'Sorry, son. Try the Technology Fair.'

The lift doors opened and the little crowd drew respectfully aside. An expensively dressed, foreign-looking lady emerged, followed by a boy of about twelve in a formal suit. They were flanked by a big man carrying a chauffeur's cap and an even bigger man who looked like a bodyguard.

Cameras clicked and flashed as the little group swept through the foyer and out of the hotel.

Michael turned to the man next to him, a suave-looking type in a trench-coat. 'Who are that lot?'

'Prince Nikolai of Syldavia and his mother. He's going home to be crowned next week.' The man took a complicated-looking pocket-knife from his pocket. 'If you need a pair of pliers, there are some on this.'

'Thanks. That's really kind of you, Mr . . .?'

'The name's Appleby. George Appleby. Leave the knife at reception when you've done with it.'

Michael took the pocket knife back to the stand and stood watching while Rex used the pliers to strip a wire and connect it to another wire inside the box.

'He was really cool, you know.'

'Who?'

'Appleby, the guy who lent me that knife.'

'Put your finger on there, will you?' said Rex.

Michael held down the wire while Rex tightened a connection.

'Do you know you're scratching?'

Rex scratched his neck. 'I'm what?'

'Scratching, as in turning into a dog. Better get under the table, quick.'

'You'll have to finish it!' Rex hissed. He dropped out of sight.

As Michael stared into the box, a small, shaggy dog with a futuristic watch strapped to its right forepaw slipped out from under the table and started to sneak away.

'Hang on, Rex,' called Michael. 'Do I just check all the circuits?'

'Woof!'

Michael held up a couple of loose wires. 'What happens here? Is it red to the left?'

'Woof! Woof!'

'Black on the left. Right!'

An angry voice called, 'What is that dog doing in here?'
here?'

Rex looked up and saw the organizer lady marching towards him. He dodged round her and streaked out through the door.

'A dog?' said Michael with an astonished air. 'I'd better go and check up.'

Giving the organizer a reassuring smile, he hurried after Rex.

Rex trotted into foyer – and ran straight into the hall porter. Waving his arms in a shooing motion, the porter edged Rex towards the door.

Michael arrived in time to see what was happening.

'Hey, I think that's my dog!' he called.

The distracted hall porter looked around – and Rex dodged past. The hall porter glared at Michael. 'He's yours, is he?'

'Actually mine's more sort of browny and he's got shorter legs. Sorry . . .'

Rex meanwhile was making a dash for the open doors of a lift. Once inside, he leapt up and stabbed at a button with his paw. The doors slid closed and he relaxed, panting a little.

An amused voice said, 'You've done this before, I take it?'

Rex looked up and saw a suave-looking man in a trench-coat.

The lift rose smoothly upwards and then stopped. The doors opened and Rex trotted out.

With a faintly puzzled smile, the man who called himself Appleby watched him disappear along the deserted corridor. The doors closed and the lift went on its way.

*

Michael was standing by the lifts wondering what to do next when Mrs Jessop appeared. She was carrying a tray which held two bottles of fizzy orange, with straws, and a cup of coffee.

'Where are you going, Michael?'

'Nowhere, miss.'

'Shall we go back and help Rex then?'

'Rex had to go, miss.'

'Where?'

'To the toilet.'

'Well, I'm sure he can manage on his own. Now, off you go!'

Reluctantly Michael headed back towards the Technology Fair.

Rex was trotting along the corridor when he ran straight into a hotel valet, who yelled, 'Hey, you!' and tried to grab him.

Rex turned and scampered back the other way. The valet pounded after him.

Rex turned a corner and ran along a wider corridor – only to find it blocked by yet another valet. This one was wheeling a trolley, covered by a white tablecloth.

To Rex's astonishment the valet lifted one side of the tablecloth. 'Quick, under here!'

Rex looked up and saw that the valet was in fact the man he'd seen in the lift, his trench-coat changed for a valet's uniform.

Puzzled, but grateful, Rex jumped on to the little shelf at the bottom of the trolley. The man lowered the cloth just as the valet who was chasing him appeared round the corner.

'Have you seen a dog?' the valet gasped. 'Fluffy, about so big?'

Appleby shook his head. ''Fraid not.'

The valet ran on, disappearing round the next corner.

Appleby wheeled the trolley up to a bedroom door, which he opened with a pass key. Pushing the trolley inside, he closed the door behind him.

He lifted the tablecloth. 'Okay, you're safe now.'

Rex jumped off the trolley, ran to the door and whined to be let out.

'Better wait till the coast's clear,' Appleby advised. He looked carefully round the room. It was a small but luxurious bedroom with armchairs and a desk as well as a bed. He went to the door that connected this room to the next, looked inside, then closed the door.

Then he went to the phone and began unscrewing the mouthpiece. Head cocked, Rex watched him insert a miniaturized electronic device. He was planting a bug!

Appleby looked up and saw the little dog watching him.

'Just keeping in touch with what's going on. Can't stand outside the door all day . . .' He replaced the mouthpiece. 'Not everyone wishes the Prince as well as we do.'

There was a tap on the door. Appleby put a finger to his lips and pointed to the bed. Obediently Rex scurried beneath it.

Appleby crossed to the window, opened it and produced a miniature grappling hook round which was coiled a fine nylon rope. Leaning out of the window, he whirled the grappling iron until it caught on the balcony of the room above, tested it with a pull, then climbed rapidly out of sight.

The room door opened and two thuggish-looking men came in. One of them, evidently the leader, opened the connecting door, then nodded in satisfaction.

'This is the room. We wait in our room till he gets back.'

The two men left, closing the door behind them.

Rex came out from under the bed. He sat on the floor and began to scratch . . .

In the Technology Fair, Michael was still working on the exhibit, glancing up at the door every few minutes.

Mrs Jessop came over. 'Well, where is he?'

'Still in the toilet, miss.'

'He's been in there an hour!'

'I'll go and see if he's all right, shall I, miss?' said Michael.

He hurried from the room.

Mrs Jessop sighed. 'If he's not, we'll need a medical team and a fire hose . . .'

Wrapped in a hotel towel, Rex, now back in human shape, wandered round the sitting room. He went to the connecting door, opened it and went through. He found himself in a huge room with a massive, canopied bed. Although Rex didn't know it, he was in the hotel's royal suite.

Rex walked over to the built-in wardrobe and looked inside. He saw a whole rack of suits, with matching shirts, underwear, even shoes and socks.

Rex took one suit off the rack and held it up against

himself. It was cut in a semi-military style with lots of gold braid. Still, it would have to do till he could reach his own things. Quickly he began to dress.

Michael was waiting by the lifts, planning to search the hotel till he found Rex. The lift arrived and its doors opened, revealing Appleby in his trench-coat.

Michael took out the super pocket-knife and handed it to him. 'Might as well give you this back now, sir. Thanks very much.'

Appleby pocketed the knife. 'Shouldn't you be off at your Technology Fair?'

'I'm looking for my friend – I mean, my dog.'

'Shaggy little animal? Is he yours?'

'Have you seen him?'

'I rescued him from the hotel staff.' Appleby glanced at his watch. 'He's quite safe – take you to him, if you like.'

Michael got in the lift.

The door to the royal suite opened and Rex appeared, looking impressive in his gold-braided suit. He looked cautiously to left and right and then hurried away along the corridor.

Appleby paused by the door to the royal suite, pulled back his sleeve, and extended a little aerial from his watch. He listened for a moment, then slid the aerial back in place.

'All clear inside.' He produced a key and opened the door.

'Are you a secret agent?' Michael asked in awed tones.

'I just – keep an eye on things.'

'It's brilliant you finding my dog,' said Michael as they entered the room. 'Except he's not really supposed to be here.'

'Why did you bring him?'

'I didn't, he just turned up. He's very intelligent, you see.'

'He is indeed,' said Appleby, looking around. 'He's managed to escape from a locked room. Unless . . .'

'Unless what?'

'Those goons who came in – they must have let him out.'

'What goons?'

'Just some people I'm keeping an eye on.'

'What sort of people?' Michael persisted.

'Nothing for you to worry about.'

'I think I'd better go and find him, all the same.' Michael paused by the door. 'He'll be all right? These people – they won't hurt him?'

Appleby shook his head. 'There's only one person they want . . .'

As Rex walked along the corridor in his gold-braided suit, a door near by opened a little and two sinister-looking men peered out. They were the 'goons' Appleby had mentioned. Their names were Gruznik and Karsh.

'It's him,' whispered Karsh. 'The Prince. He must have come back early. Get Jakob!'

Unaware that he was being followed, Rex wandered along the endless hotel corridors.

Behind him the three men started to close in. They were about to pounce when a hotel valet came round the corner. The baffled goons fell back.

The valet saw Rex and bowed. 'Can I assist Your Excellency?'

'Can you tell me the way to the Technology Fair?'

The valet bowed again. 'If Your Excellency will follow me?'

Rex followed the valet and the three thugs trailed Rex.

Suddenly Michael appeared round a corner. 'Rex!'

Rex turned to the valet. 'I'll be okay now, thanks.'

The valet bowed and moved away.

'Amazing place, this,' said Rex. 'They treat you like royalty!'

'Mrs Jessop is after you,' said Michael. 'She thinks you've been in the loo for the last three-quarters of an hour!'

'I'd better get back down there.'

'Not in that comic opera outfit you don't,' said Michael. 'Where did you get it from anyway?'

'Had to borrow it – bit of an emergency.'

'Wait here and I'll get your proper clothes.'

Michael hurried away and the three thugs re-appeared. Karsh and Gruznik were carrying a large laundry basket. As soon as Michael was out of sight they marched up to Rex, Karsh opened the lid, Jakob shoved Rex inside and they hurried away.

Back at their stand, Michael was grabbing Rex's clothes from under the table and shoving them into his school bag. As he moved away he ran straight into Mrs Jessop.

'Where do you think you're going, Michael?'

'We're testing the tracking device, miss. Rex has gone off with the bleeper.'

Mrs Jessop fixed him with her famous beady eye. 'I

want you both back here in five minutes, Michael. Five minutes – or there'll be murder!'

Michael came out of the lift and ran to the place where he'd left Rex – but Rex was nowhere to be seen. Michael hesitated for a moment, then ran back to the lifts.

Rex meanwhile was in the thugs' hotel room, with two of the three thugs standing over him. The third had gone off somewhere. Rex was tied to a chair, though his right arm was still free.

Karsh placed a document on a little table in front of Rex and put a pen in his free hand. 'Sign!'

'Why?' Rex asked.

'Just sign!'

'What happens if I do?'

'You will no longer be king, but you will be free.'

'I won't be king?'

'It is regrettable, but that will not be possible,' Karsh said stiffly.

'You'll let me go, though? Even though I can't be king?'

'We shall!'

'All right,' said Rex, 'I'll sign. I never wanted to be king much anyway!'

Michael raced back into the room where the Technology Fair was being held, ran to their table, grabbed one of the boxes and hurried back the way he had come. On his way out he shot past an astonished Mrs Jessop.

'Still testing!' Michael announced brightly, and sped on his way.

As Michael went out, the Prince, his mother, his chauffeur and his bodyguard all came into the room. The Prince looked around for someone in authority and, naturally, his eye fell on Mrs Jessop.

'My mother asks if you will show me something of your most interesting science exhibition?'

'I'm afraid there's very little time before the judging . . .'

'But you will show me?' said the Prince with a charming smile.

Clearly, there was no escape.

'It will be a pleasure, Your Excellency,' said Mrs Jessop.

Michael came out of the lift and stood in the corridor. He switched on the box, the light glowed and there was a faint hum. He set off to the left. The light dimmed and the hum became even fainter.

He turned and moved in the opposite direction. The light glowed brighter and the hum became more high-pitched . . .

Rex finished scrawling a large and quite illegible signature at the bottom of the document. 'Is that it, then? Will you untie me, please?'

For a moment he thought he was going to be freed – but instead Karsh finished tying him up, so that his right arm was no longer free. 'We must wait till our leader, Colonel Saparov, arrives. Gruznik has gone to find him.'

'So you're not letting me go?'

'Not yet,' Karsh replied.

There was a tap on the door and a high-pitched voice called, 'Room service! The meals you ordered.'

'One moment,' said Karsh.

He nodded to Jakob, who grabbed the back of Rex's chair and dragged it through the connecting door into the other room.

Karsh opened the door and a rather tall maid came in, pushing a food-laden trolley. She reached for the coffee pot and twisted its lid – and the room was suddenly filled with choking white smoke.

The maid flung open the connecting door, saw Rex tied to the chair, and said in Appleby's voice: 'Shan't be a sec!'

Jakob sprang forward and Appleby felled him with a single karate chop. Karsh moved in to the attack and Appleby threw him across the room.

Working like a charm, the tracker had brought Michael to the very door of Karsh's room. He stood outside, the light glowing brightly and the 'ping' at its loudest . . .

Unfortunately, Colonel Saparov had been delayed, and Gruznik had decided to check up on his prisoner. He came along the corridor and was surprised to see a boy with a flashing, pinging box outside his room. Gruznik drew his gun and thrust it in the boy's back.

'Now open the door – slowly.'

Michael opened the door.

'Nobody move,' Gruznik shouted, 'or the boy dies!'

They both went inside.

Mrs Jessop was explaining the tracker device to the Prince and his entourage. It was a little hard to demonstrate with half her apparatus and both her assistants missing.

'Fascinating!' said the Prince. 'Now please explain again more slowly for the benefit of my mother. Her English is not good.'

Mrs Jessop gritted her teeth. 'An honour, Your Excellency.'

Rex was still tied to a chair in the inner room, but now he had company. Appleby and Michael were tied to chairs as well, one on each side of him.

Gruznik was covering them with his gun. Jakob and Karsh were with him, bruised but no longer unconscious.

'Sorry about all this,' Appleby was saying. 'I couldn't risk trying anything once he had that gun on you.'

'It's all my fault,' Michael said miserably.

'No problem,' said Appleby. 'Soon have you out of here.'

'I think not,' Karsh snarled. 'Gruznik, take him next door and stay with him. Jakob, stand guard in the corridor. I shall go to meet Colonel Saparov. He should be here by now.'

Gruznik dragged Appleby into the outer room. Jakob and Karsh left, and Michael and Rex were left alone. Michael saw that Rex was wriggling desperately . . .

By now the judging had started and the little group of judges had reached Mrs Jessop's stand. Seeing the Prince, they naturally assumed he was a competitor.

'Perhaps you would like to explain your project, young man?' one of the judges said.

There was a shocked gasp from the Prince's entourage – but the Prince smiled and said, 'I should be delighted . . .'

Mrs Jessop thought he made a very good job of it.

Michael was still tied to his chair, but Rex, now a dog once more, was wriggling free of the ropes and his borrowed clothes.

'What's got into you?' Michael whispered. 'You're changing back and forth like a yo-yo. Must be all the excitement!'

Rex licked his hand and crept silently over to the connecting door, which was a little ajar. Pushing it open with his nose, Rex peered into the room.

Appleby was lashed to his chair and Gruznik was stretched out on the sofa, watching cartoons on the television.

Rex wriggled round the edge of the room till he could get behind Appleby. He began gnawing at the ropes that tied the man to his chair.

Soon the ropes began dropping away and Appleby gradually worked himself free. He leapt to his feet and hurled himself upon the unfortunate Gruznik, who was overpowered before he knew what was happening. Taking a pair of handcuffs from the heel of his shoe, Appleby handcuffed him to the radiator.

He went into the next room, where Rex had already freed Michael from his bonds.

Appleby looked at the empty chair beside Michael.

'Where's he gone?'

'Er – to the bathroom,' said Michael.

Appleby nodded. 'Safest place for him.' He went over to the door and listened. 'There's a goon outside,' he whispered. 'I need to get him in here.'

Rex ran to the door and started barking loudly. Jakob opened the door and came in, gun in hand. Appleby leapt from behind the door, immobilized him with a quick judo hold, disarmed him, and handcuffed him with a second pair of handcuffs from his other shoe. He marched him into the next room.

'Two down, and two to go!'

A tall, brutal-looking man in an elaborate uniform came into the hotel foyer. He was Colonel Saparov, Syldavia's Chief of Police and the secret leader of the conspirators. Karsh was waiting to meet him. They headed for the lift.

The Prince was getting carried away by his role.

'Now I have explained, perhaps you would like a demonstration?'

He picked up the remaining box and switched it on. The lights flashed and there was a low pinging sound.

'A signal!' the Prince cried. 'Let us see where it is coming from! Follow me, everyone!'

He marched out of the room with his entourage and the judges following behind.

Proudly Karsh showed Colonel Saparov into his hotel room. For some reason the room was in semi-darkness. But Saparov could see the Prince tied to a chair, his back to the door and his head slumped despairingly.

'Excellent!' he said.

'Thank you, Colonel,' Karsh said humbly.

'You will now take the Prince out by the kitchen entrance to my waiting van, which will convey you to the airfield. By this evening Prince Nikolai will be my prisoner, and I shall be President of Syldavia.'

Suddenly the lights came on, and the Prince stood up. Except, of course, that it wasn't the Prince, it was Appleby. He pulled back his sleeve to reveal a miniature tape-recorder. He switched it on and Saparov's voice rang out:

'By this evening Prince Nikolai will be my prisoner, and I shall be President of Syldavia.'

'I'm sure the Prince will be interested to hear of your ambitions, Colonel,' Appleby said.

Colonel Saparov seemed stunned, but Karsh pulled out a gun. A small, shaggy dog leapt, panther-like, from the top of the wardrobe, knocking the gun out of Karsh's hand.

Rex picked up the gun in his teeth and brought it over to Appleby, who said, 'Good thinking, dog!'

Karsh and the colonel turned to run, but Michael, who had been working the light switch, suddenly heard a familiar pinging sound.

He flung open the door to reveal the Prince, the real Prince. He was clutching a box: it had lights on it and gave out a loud, repeated, pinging sound.

'Ah, Colonel Saparov,' said the Prince. 'Let me show you this remarkable machine, made by boys of my own age!'

As the the colonel and his henchmen were being taken away by the police, Appleby bent down and patted Rex.

'He really is a most remarkable dog.'

'I'm still in trouble, though,' said Michael. 'The batteries have run down, so I can't demonstrate our machine. Then there's my dog. He's not supposed to be here, but all sorts of people have seen him. My teacher's going to kill me.'

'Then we must find a good reason for the dog to be here.'

'What reason can there be?'

'I have an idea,' said Appleby. 'We'll need some materials from the hotel store room and we'll have to work fast. But I think we can solve all your problems in one go.'

The judging had been resumed and Michael was being given a chance to demonstrate his invention.

'I decided at the last minute that this would be more environmentally friendly,' he said. 'That's why I used the dog.'

The judges were looking at a miniature treadmill made out of cardboard tube rollers on a wooden base. Around the rollers was stretched a continuous cloth belt to which thin wooden slats had been fixed. The whole contraption was linked to one of the wooden boxes. On top of the treadmill sat a small shaggy dog.

At a signal from Michael, the little dog stood up and started to trot. The treadmill rolled around, the lights on the box lit up and it started giving out a series of pings.

The judges all started to applaud, Michael sighed with relief – and Rex gave a triumphant 'Woof!'

Green Eye of the Little Yellow Dog

There was good news and bad news on Rex Thomas's birthday. The good news was, he got the huge kite he'd been hoping for. The bad news was, his dad got a letter saying that their landlord was selling up and they'd have to find a new site for Mr Thomas's sports shop.

Rex told Michael about it in a quiet corner of the playground.

'It spoiled things a bit. I wanted him to fly the kite with me tomorrow, but now he'll be going round estate agents. We never get a chance to do anything together.'

'Never mind,' said Michael. 'Maybe this'll cheer you up.' He handed Rex a small, untidy parcel wrapped in coloured paper. 'Happy birthday!'

Rex opened the parcel and discovered a foam-rubber squeaky animal in a particularly vile shade of pink. He sighed and hurriedly wrapped it up again. 'Thanks a lot, Michael. Very funny!'

'You'll like it when you're a dog!'

Mrs Jessop drifted past on playground duty and noticed the parcel. 'What's all this, then?'

'It's Rex's birthday, miss.'

'Happy birthday, Rex. What's he given you?'

Reluctantly Rex handed her the parcel.

She unwrapped it, looked inside, shuddered and wrapped it up again. 'A squeaky dog toy! Is it just what you always wanted, Rex?'

'Oh yes, miss.'

'That's good then . . .' She wandered away.

After school, Rex and Michael took the kite out on the common. It was huge once it was assembled. Rex wondered if they'd ever get it off the ground.

Michael held up the kite while Rex backed away, reeling out the line. He got as far away as he could, which took him as far as the hedge round the car park. Something moved at his feet and he looked down.

'Michael!' he called. 'Over here!'

Michael put down the kite and ran over to join him.

Rex pointed downwards. There, fast asleep under the hedge, was a tiny puppy.

'Wow!' said Michael softly.

Rex bent down and picked the puppy up gently. It wriggled and licked his face.

They left the common and headed for home, Rex carrying the puppy and Michael the kite.

'We couldn't leave it,' said Rex. 'It might have died. Could have been eaten by a fox or anything.'

'We had no choice,' said Michael. 'We're just being responsible, like Mrs Jessop is always telling us.'

Rex sighed. 'Dad's going to hate this . . .'

Mr Thomas held the puppy and stroked it gently. 'You're gorgeous, aren't you?' He put it down gently on the rug.

Rex and Michael looked at each other.

'Can we keep him?' asked Rex.

'We'll have to tell the police, of course,' said Mr Thomas. 'He's a West Highland terrier, could be quite valuable. But if him no one claims him ... Well, I don't see why not.'

Michael and Rex gave the puppy some food and some water on a newspaper in the corner. It drank a little water but left most of the food.

'He can have Bob's old basket,' said Michael. 'The one that's too small.'

'I've already got a toy for him,' said Rex.

The doorbell rang.

'That'll be Mrs Jessop,' said Mr Thomas. 'We're having a conference about school cricket.'

Cricket was forgotten while Mrs Jessop cooed over the puppy. 'Look at those little paws! You should call him Moses!'

Michael looked puzzled. 'Did Moses have little feet, miss?'

'Not that we know of.'

'He was found in a clump of bulrushes,' said Rex.

'No he wasn't,' said Michael. 'We found him in the hedge by the car park.'

'Not the dog – Moses, you twit.' Suddenly Rex started to scratch. He moved towards the door. 'Think it's time I was off to bed. Goodnight, everyone.'

'Is Rex all right?' Mrs Jessop asked.

'He often comes over like that,' said Mr Thomas. 'One minute he's chatting away, the next he's flaked out and ready for bed.'

'I'd better be going as well,' said Michael. 'See you, Mr Thomas, 'night, miss.'

He followed Rex out.

A few minutes later, a small shaggy dog came into the room.

'Hello, Bob,' said Mr Thomas. 'Didn't know you were around.'

'Will he be all right with the puppy?' Mrs Jessop wondered.

'I'm sure he will, he's a very gentle dog.'

They watched as the little dog moved across to the puppy. Its lips curled back and it growled menacingly.

'Easy now, Bob,' said Mr Thomas. 'He'll be a friend for you too, you know.'

The little dog growled again.

'He's probably a bit worried about his territory,' said Mrs Jessop. 'I'm sure they'll settle down.'

There was a sudden snarl and the puppy scurried under Mr Thomas's chair. Mr Thomas and Mrs Jessop watched as the dog went over to the corner, ate all the puppy's food and drank all the water. Then it advanced on the puppy, still growling.

'I'll take him out, just in case,' said Mr Thomas, grabbing the dog by the scruff of its neck. 'Come on, out you go!'

He took the dog along the landing and opened the door of Rex's room. 'You stay in there with Rex for a bit. And next time, behave!' He shoved the dog inside and closed the door.

'I can't believe it,' Rex said, next day in the playground. 'I was so jealous!'

'But it's no threat to you,' said Michael.

'I don't know what came over me,' said Rex. 'I behaved like a real . . .'

'Dog?' Michael suggested.

Rex nodded miserably. 'What am I going to do? I don't understand it. When I'm the way I am now, I just love having the puppy. When I'm a dog, all I do is growl at it . . .'

Mr Thomas was worried too. 'Bob really had a go at the puppy last night,' he told Rex when he got home. He was pretty serious about it. 'I hope we're not going to have trouble.'

But they did. Later that evening, Mr Thomas heard terrible growling coming from the kitchen. He ran into the room to find Moses the puppy cowering in the corner while the little dog methodically ripped its basket and blanket to pieces. The destruction complete, the dog advanced, growling on the puppy.

Mr Thomas dashed across the room and scooped up the angry little dog. 'That's it, out you go!' He carried the dog downstairs, opened the front door and put it out into the street.

Rex the dog scurried down the alley beside the house. Following his usual route, he jumped on a dustbin, up on to the wall, from the wall to the extension roof, and from there through his bedroom window.

He crawled miserably under the bed and just lay there for a while. After some time he started to scratch.

Rex had just finished getting into bed when his father came into the room, his face grave. 'Bob's just gone for Moses again.'

'Oh no!'

'He really went for him this time. I'm afraid he might kill him if we don't do something.'

'He wouldn't!'

'I'm afraid he's going to have to go,' said Mr
Thomas sadly.

Rex sighed. 'Poor puppy.'

'I mean Bob,' said Mr Thomas.

'Bob?' said Rex, horrified. 'But he can't go!'

'We could find him a good home, somewhere with
no other dogs. He'd probably be happier.'

'You can't throw Bob out. This is his home!'

'Well, not really, he comes and goes. He's a stray.'

'We should try and understand him,' Rex said desperately. 'He's upset!'

'You talk as if he was human,' said Mr Thomas.
'You go to sleep. I'll sort it all out, it's not your
problem. Sleep well.'

Rex slumped back on his pillow in despair.

'He's going to get rid of me,' he told Michael next day
in the playground.

'But he can't!'

'I tore up the puppy's bedclothes and ate his basket!
If I was him, *I'd* get rid of me.'

'Why did you do it?'

'I don't know ... When I'm a dog, I don't think
like a person any more. I think like a dog. Things are
very simple when you're a dog. You like things or you
bite them!'

Michael thought for a moment. 'Perhaps you could
persuade him to get rid of the puppy instead?'

'I've tried, but he won't. It's a poor, defenceless
little thing, and I'm just a stray.'

'He won't get rid of you,' said Michael. 'He's bound
to give you another chance.'

Mrs Jessop came up to them. 'I've just been talking

to your father, Rex. You're going to get a bit of peace at last. Bob's coming to live with me!'

For once Rex was speechless.

That evening, Mr Thomas drove round to Mrs Jessop's house and handed over a dog basket, a feeding bowl and a very fed-up-looking, small, shaggy dog.

He and Mrs Jessop stood chatting for a moment on the front doorstep.

'This is very good of you,' he said. 'I thought of getting rid of the puppy, but Rex adores him. He's never taken much notice of Bob, doesn't play with him or take him for walks. I can hardly ever remember seeing them together!'

'I'm sure we'll be fine,' said Mrs Jessop. 'Won't we, Bob?'

The dog sighed.

'Remember, he's really a stray,' said Mr Thomas. 'He tends to come and go a bit . . .'

'There was just one thing,' said Mrs Jessop. 'Have you got a name-tag for him?'

'We've got one somewhere, but he doesn't like to wear it.'

'I'd sooner he did,' Mrs Jessop said firmly.

'I'll get Rex to drop it round to you. Well, goodbye for now.'

'Goodbye.'

Mr Thomas bent down. 'Goodbye, Bob.'

The little dog gave him a disgusted look and followed Mrs Jessop into the house.

Later that evening, Mrs Jessop sat marking exercise books at the kitchen table. Rex lay stretched out on the floor, looking utterly miserable.

Mrs Jessop glanced down at him. 'Cheer up, I'm not that bad. You mustn't believe everything the children tell you.'

The little dog started to scratch. Mrs Jessop went back to her books and the dog sneaked out of the room.

He trotted along to Mrs Jessop's utility room, where his dog basket was kept in a nice warm spot near the boiler. He tugged off the blanket with his teeth, revealing a pile of boy's clothes hidden at the bottom of the basket . . .

Some time later, Rex, back in his boy shape, crept along the landing towards his bedroom. The kitchen door opened and his father looked out.

'Rex? Why are you up so late?'

'I was getting a drink of water,' said Rex. 'I couldn't sleep, I was worrying about the dog.'

Mr Thomas threw down the morning mail in disgust.

'Not a single new shop in the post – and I'm on the mailing lists of five agencies.'

'I could have a look for you, when I'm taking Bob for his walks.'

'Don't worry about Bob, Mrs Jessop is looking after him now. Oh, I said you'd take his dog-tag round. Maybe you ought to buy him a collar and lead as well. I'll give you the money.'

'Good idea,' said Rex thoughtfully. 'I'll do it straight away.'

Anyone watching Rex's actions that afternoon would have thought he was acting rather strangely. The lead was no problem, but he had to go into several pet shops before he found exactly the kind of collar he wanted.

Then he went to an ironmonger's shop and bought a length of stiff but bendy wire exactly the same length as the lead . . .

Rex rang Mrs Jessop's doorbell and she came to the door in her leisure-time costume of jeans and a sweat-shirt. She was carrying her newspaper.

'I've brought Bob's name-tag round,' said Rex. He held up a broad elastic collar with a name-tag attached.

'Elastic? Haven't seen one like this before.'

'He doesn't like anything tight round his neck, miss. I was wondering if I could take him for a walk.'

'If you can find him. He disappeared earlier, but he might be in his basket in the utility room.' She ushered Rex into the house. 'It's down there, on the left.'

She went back into the kitchen.

In the utility room Rex pulled the elastic collar over his own head. He took out the lead, which now had a length of wire running along its centre. When he stretched out the lead, it stayed out, as if being pulled taut by an invisible dog.

Mrs Jessop was pouring herself another cup of coffee when she heard a yell of 'Here, boy! Good dog!'

She opened the window and looked out, catching a brief glimpse of Rex dashing past. 'You found him then?' she called.

Rex reappeared round the end of the building. He was holding one end of the stretched-out lead. Obviously it was being pulled hard by the enthusiastic dog, which was just out of sight round the corner.

'Yes, miss,' Rex replied. 'We're just off for a walk. He's very keen.' He disappeared round the corner, yanked out of sight by the unseen dog.

Mrs Jessop smiled and went back to her newspaper.

A little later she saw a ball thrown over her garden hedge.

Rex ran into the garden and picked it up, giving her a wave.

On the other side of the hedge, Rex started to scratch. He threw the ball . . .

Mrs Jessop heard excited barking and saw the dog Bob dash into the garden and retrieve the ball. A few minutes later he trotted into the kitchen with it in his mouth.

'Hello, boy,' she said. 'Have a nice game?'

She patted his head, pleased to see he was wearing his elastic collar and name-tag. Obviously worn out, the little dog stretched out in the corner and went to sleep.

Several hours later, the dog woke up. Mrs Jessop had gone off somewhere and he was alone in the kitchen. He looked at the clock and saw with alarm that it was nearly six. The dog jumped up and ran out of the room.

After a frantic cross-town dash, Rex reached his house and came in by his usual route through the bedroom window.

In the kitchen Mr Thomas put two plates of fish fingers and chips on the table.

'Supper, Rex!' he called.

Rex hurried into the kitchen, still pulling on his T-shirt. He nodded to his father, slumped down at the table and began wolfing down his food.

Worriedly, Mr Thomas watched him eat.

It was next morning and Mr Thomas was standing on the landing in his dressing gown, rapping on the bathroom door.

'Rex? Are you going to be much longer?'

A grunting sound that *might* have meant 'No' came from behind the door, mixed with the sound of rushing water. Mr Thomas sighed and went back to his bedroom.

Inside the bathroom, Rex, now back in his dog shape, jumped up to the shower control and turned it off with his paw.

A little later, Mr Thomas came out of his bedroom to try again.

The bathroom door stood open and a trail of water led along the landing to Rex's room.

'Boys!' said Mr Thomas.

Meanwhile a very small and very wet dog dashed out of the alleyway and hurtled along the pavement. It crossed the road at the traffic lights, tore along several side streets and whizzed into Mrs Jessop's driveway.

Mrs Jessop finished her tea and toast, put down her newspaper and went along to the utility room. Bob the dog lay, panting, in his basket.

'Morning, Bob!' she said cheerfully.

'You know, I've been thinking,' said Michael, as they walked to school. 'What you need to do is to show your dad and Mrs Jessop that you're missing yourself – missing Bob, I mean.'

'That's what I'm trying to do,' said Rex wearily. '*And* be in two places at the same time, *and* find my dad a new shop. It's not easy . . .'

'Risky, too, I should think,' said Michael. 'I mean, what if something goes wrong?'

Something went wrong the very next night.

Rex had finished his evening stint as Bob the dog at Mrs Jessop's, and had trotted home again. He followed his usual route to his bedroom window – and found it closed.

He stood up and pushed at it with his paws, but it wouldn't budge. Sadly Rex ran back across the roof and made his way down to the ground.

As he came out of the alleyway it was already beginning to rain. Sad and homeless, Rex trotted along the street. No use going back to Mrs Jessop's house, she kept the place well locked up. He turned into a shop doorway and tried to settle down for the night. The rain got heavier and thunder rumbled across the sky.

Suddenly Rex heard a terrifying growl. In a flash of lightning he saw a huge, terrifying, black dog galloping towards him.

Rex abandoned his doorway and ran for it, the big dog growling and snapping at his heels.

It was a nightmare chase through the thunderstorm, with the fierce dog always close behind. Rex ran along street after street until he was in a completely strange part of town. All the time the big dog was coming closer.

Rex could feel himself tiring, and he knew he

couldn't keep going much longer. As he ran down an alleyway behind a little row of shops, he saw a broken ground-floor window and went through it in a flying leap.

The gap was far too small for the big dog to get through. It barked at the window for a time, then gave up and went away.

Too tired even to worry about where he was, Rex curled up in a corner and fell asleep.

Early next morning, Rex let himself out of the door of an empty shop. He was wearing a pair of ancient wellies that were full of holes and a long, brown, storeman's coat which came down to his ankles. He'd woken up as a boy in the morning, and had been glad to find something – anything – to wear for the journey home.

When he got back to his house, he jumped up on the dustbin, walked along the wall, climbed over the roof and got in through his bedroom window – luckily it had just been closed, not locked, and in human form it was easy enough to open.

He got washed and dressed and came down late to breakfast. His father was just about to take Moses for an early-morning walk.

Rex swallowed a quick cup of tea and went with him.

'I've got some brilliant news, Dad,' he said as they walked along. 'I found this place yesterday, when I was out for a walk with Bob. I think it might do for your new shop.'

'Well, well,' said Mr Thomas. 'And where is this place?'

Rex looked blank.

'Do you know what street it's in?'

'Er . . .' Suddenly Rex had an idea. 'It's all right, Dad,' he said. 'Bob will know!'

An old man came out of the shop where Rex had spent the night and closed the door carefully behind him. He heard a pitiful whine and looked down to see a small, shaggy dog crouched in the doorway.

He bent down to pat it. 'You all right, boy? You don't look all right.'

He bent down and checked the dog's identity-disc.

'You're a long way from home, aren't you? Come on, I'll take you back in the car. I only came in to check up on the shop. Someone's broken a window . . .'

The old man led Rex to an old car, parked at the kerb, and opened the back door. 'Jump in!'

It was only a short drive home and, when they arrived, Rex led the old man into the shop. His father was in the little office behind the counter, sorting through a pile of estate agents' brochures and looking worried.

The old man introduced himself – his name was Goodall – and explained about finding the dog.

'Very kind of you,' said Mr Thomas.

'No trouble at all,' said Mr Goodall.

As the two men chatted, Rex jumped up with his front paws on the desk and knocked over the pile of brochures. He shoved them towards the two men, then sat down again next to Mr Thomas.

Mr Goodall looked at the brochures. 'Looking for a shop, are you? Now there's a coincidence! I've just retired and I've got this place on my hands . . .'

*

Mrs Jessop opened her front door to find Mr Thomas on her doorstep, a small, shaggy dog at his heels.

'Come in,' she said.

'I won't if you don't mind. Got a lot to do, moving the stuff to the new shop. I just wanted to thank you for looking after Bob here.'

'I really enjoyed it.'

'I'm sorry we had to take him back, but Rex missed him so.'

Mrs Jessop nodded. 'He deserves to have him back. He was always round here, taking him for walks, playing games . . .'

'Anyway, I've got something for you,' said Mr Thomas. 'In case you feel lonely without him.'

He reached under his coat and produced Moses the puppy.

'We'd like you to have him.'

Mrs Jessop took the little puppy and cuddled it. She was obviously very pleased. 'I don't know what to say. I must admit I've got used to having a dog.'

'Well, I'd better be going,' said Mr Thomas.

The little dog jumped up and sniffed at the puppy.

'I think he's all right now,' said Mrs Jessop. She held out the puppy, and the dog licked its face. 'Well, good luck in the new shop. I'll be along to check up on you.'

Mr Thomas said goodbye and went on his way, Rex trotting at his heels.

When the fuss of the move was over, Rex and Michael went on the common to have another go at flying Rex's birthday kite.

As before, Michael held the kite and Rex walked away with the string. When he reached the hedge, he instinctively glanced down.

'There's not another one, is there?' Michael called.

Rex shook his head. 'No puppies, no distractions. This time nothing can go wrong.'

Michael threw the kite in the air and Rex began to run, pulling the taut string. Rex ran faster and faster and the kite rose higher and higher.

Rex disappeared from Michael's view behind a small clump of trees and the huge kite rose higher still.

In fact, thought Michael, it was rising alarmingly fast. 'Rex,' he called, 'are you all right?'

The kite rose over the trees, and suddenly Michael saw beneath the kite a small shaggy dog dangling high in the air, holding on to the string with its teeth.

'Oh no!' said Michael.

From high in the air came a distant, worried 'Woooooof!'

High Temperatures

Rex was sitting at the little desk in his room making entries in a notebook. 'Wednesday', Rex wrote. 'D – 09.43–14.17.'

The entries seemed to cover most of the last few days. Some time-periods were marked 'D', others 'B'. There were a lot more Ds than Bs.

There was a tap at the door, and Rex's father stuck his head into the room. 'How are you feeling? Still woozy?'

Rex closed the notebook. 'Much better, thanks.'

'I wondered if you could look after the shop for a few minutes while I made a phone call? Of course, if you're not up to it . . .'

'No, that's fine.' Rex followed his father out of the room and went down the stairs that led down to the shop.

'By the way,' Mr Thomas called, 'I've had a letter from Great-Aunt Sarah this morning. She's asked us to go down and see her. What do you think?'

Rex's voice drifted back up the stairs. 'Yeah, sure . . .'

'That's what I like,' Mr Thomas muttered. 'Bags of enthusiasm.'

Rex was already scratching as he came into the

shop. Inevitably a customer came in at exactly that moment. She was a pleasant-looking, middle-aged woman, and she gave Rex a friendly smile. 'Good afternoon, I'm looking for a tennis racket.' She closed the door then turned back into the shop. 'I was wondering if you had anything suitable for –' She looked around in surprise. The young man behind the counter had disappeared. 'Hello? Anyone there?'

A shaggy little dog appeared from behind the counter. It trotted over to a display rack, pulled out a racket and carried it over to her.

She took the racket and examined it.

'Actually I wanted something a little smaller. It's for my daughter. Nothing too expensive, just –'

The dog sighed, took the racket from her hand and carried it back to the rack. It studied the display for a moment, selected another racket and carried it over to her.

The woman looked at it. 'Yes, that's exactly what I was looking for! Have you got a case to go with it?'

The dog brought her a case.

The woman smiled. 'You're rather good at this, aren't you? How much do I owe you?' She examined the price-tags. 'The racket's nineteen pounds eighty-seven, plus three pounds sixty for the case. That makes –'

She heard a loud 'ting' and looked up to see that the dog was sitting on a stool behind the till, pressing the keys with a paw. As she watched, it rang up twenty-three pounds forty-seven.

Mr Thomas came into the shop.

'I'm so sorry, I thought my son was here.'

'Not to worry, your little dog's been looking after

me. He found exactly what I wanted, and he's rung up the total on the till. I think you might have to help him sort out the change.'

'Yes, of course.' Mr Thomas took the woman's money and gave her the change, then he put the case and racket in a bag for her.

'He really is a remarkable dog,' the woman said. 'It must be wonderful to have someone reliable in the shop.'

'It would be,' Mr Thomas muttered.

As the woman went out, Michael came into the shop. He was carrying his schoolbag, and he had a small wart on one side of his nose.

'Morning, Mr Thomas,' said Michael. 'It's a wart. Everywhere I go, people say, "You've got a spot on your nose." It's not a spot, it's a wart, and I'd rather not talk about it. Is Rex ready? We were going swimming this afternoon.'

'I'm afraid Rex is a bit under the weather. I think he's got a temperature. I've made a doctor's appointment for him this afternoon. You wouldn't walk round to the surgery with him, would you, Michael? I've got the shop to look after, you see.'

'No problem,' said Michael. 'I'll take him now.' He opened the door for the little dog and began to leave.

'Michael,' Mr Thomas called. 'Rex is upstairs!'

'Yes, of course.' Michael turned and headed for the stairs.

'I don't suppose you know why he left his clothes here?' Mr Thomas scooped up Rex's clothes and passed them over to Michael. 'You might ask him to put them on before he leaves . . .'

*

Michael carried the clothes into Rex's room and dumped them on the bed. The little dog followed him in.

'You've been a dog rather a lot lately, haven't you?' said Michael. 'Yesterday afternoon, most of this morning . . .'

'Woof!' said Rex and jumped up at the desk, putting his paw on the notebook.

Michael opened it and studied the entries. 'You've been worrying about it too, eh?'

'Woof!'

Michael put the notebook in his bag. 'Well, first things first. I've got to get you to the doctor.'

Michael walked along the high street, Rex trotting at his side. Since Rex was still obstinately stuck in his doggy state, they'd had to sneak out without Mr Thomas seeing them.

Michael came to a halt and opened the surgery door for Rex.

Rex sat on the pavement without moving. He looked up at the sign over the door.

'Well, of course it's the vet's surgery,' said Michael. 'You can't see the ordinary doctor like that, and someone's got to check you over. Come on!'

Rex still didn't move.

'Look, I know how you feel about injections. We'll just let him have a look at you. He won't do anything else, I promise.'

Reluctantly Rex followed him inside.

Rex stood unhappily on a table in the vet's surgery, Michael standing beside him.

'We'll just check the temperature,' said the vet. He

picked up a thermometer in one hand and lifted Rex's tail with the other.

Rex growled.

'He prefers to have his temperature taken in his mouth,' Michael said hurriedly.

'Unfortunately, animals tend to bite the glass.'

'He won't bite, I promise you,' said Michael. 'It's what he's used to.'

'Well, if you're sure.' The vet put the thermometer under Rex's tongue, and the little dog held it without fuss.

'Very good,' said the vet. 'You say he's been a bit seedy?'

'He's not been himself for a couple of days. No energy, just sits around watching television.'

'Interesting!' The vet took the thermometer out of Rex's mouth. 'By the way, did you know you had a −'

'It's a wart!' said Michael wearily. 'What about my dog? Is he all right?'

The vet studied the thermometer. 'He's got a slight temperature. My guess is, he's caught a mild viral infection and it's given him a bit of a fever. It's nothing serious, just keep him at home for a bit and make sure he has plenty to drink. He'll be okay in a day or two. Now, what about booster shots? Has he had all his injections against distemper and so on?'

'Er . . .' said Michael.

'I see he hasn't,' the vet said reproachfully. 'First rule of having a dog, you know, you must make sure he has all his shots.'

'He doesn't like injections,' Michael said desperately.

The vet smiled. 'Best thing about being a dog is, you don't worry about these things in advance!'

Turning away, he picked up a large hypodermic and a vial of serum. 'Mind you, I knew a dog once . . . If you even mentioned the word "hypodermic", he used to shut himself in one of those cupboards and hold the door closed with his paw. Remarkable dog. Called Eric . . .'

Suddenly the vet realized that Rex was no longer on the table. He had shut himself in one of the surgery's glass-fronted cupboards. Bending down, the vet saw that one of the dog's paws was holding the door firmly closed.

He looked up. 'Not a relation of Eric's, is he?'

When Michael eventually managed to get Rex out of the vet's cupboard and out of his surgery, they went and sat on a bench in the shopping precinct.

Michael studied Rex's notebook. 'According to this, you've only been a boy for seventy-seven out of the last ninety-six hours. You could have a serious problem here, Rex.'

'Woof!'

'Do you have any idea why it's happening?'

'Woof! Woof!'

Still studying the notebook, Michael didn't notice that Rex had started scratching. 'Well, you'd better find out, before your life gets even more complicated than it is already. Rex?'

The little dog had leapt off the bench and was racing into the nearest shop – which happened to be a fashion boutique.

Michael hurried after him.

It was a largish shop, rather dimly lit, and Michael could see no sign of Rex among the racks of fashionable clothes on display. He caught one of the sales assistants staring at him and said sharply, 'It's a wart, all right? I wish people would just leave me alone.'

The girl looked hurt. 'I was wondering if you needed any help.'

'No thanks, I'm just looking for something for a friend.'

Michael fingered something on the nearest rack, realized it was a frilly nightie and moved hurriedly on.

He went to the very back of the shop and found himself outside a row of curtained fitting-cubicles. A woman came out, gave him a suspicious look and hurried away.

Suddenly he heard a low whisper. 'Michael? Are you there, Michael?'

'Rex? Where are you?'

Rex's head, his boy's head, popped out from the end cubicle. 'I'm in here!'

'Are you all right?'

'Of course I'm not all right! I can't walk out of here like this, can I?'

Michael looked around. 'I'll try to find you something. What's your size? Don't want anything too tight, do we? What about colour?'

'Are you expecting me to wear a dress?'

'I'm not sure you have any choice, Rex!'

'Haven't you got anything in your bag?'

'Of course, the bag,' said Michael. 'Good thinking! Here, help yourself!'

He passed the bag over and Rex vanished behind the curtains.

A few minutes later, Michael walked out of the shop. Rex was beside him, tastefully dressed in swimming trunks and flippers, with a towel over his shoulder.

He smiled politely at the salesgirls by the cash desk. 'Thank you very much. A little too expensive for us, I'm afraid.'

Mr Thomas looked up as Rex and Michael came into the shop.

'How did you get on with the doctor?'

'Mild virus infection,' said Rex. 'Nothing to worry about. It'll probably clear up by itself in a few days.'

'Well, that's a relief. Dr Townshend, was it?'

'It was a different doctor today,' said Michael. 'Nice man, very helpful.'

The two boys headed for the stairs.

Mr Thomas hesitated for a moment. 'Rex, I don't suppose you want to tell me why you're wearing –'

But it was too late. Rex and Michael had vanished upstairs.

In Rex's bedroom, Michael studied the figures in the notebook while Rex finished getting dressed. 'I make it seventy-seven hours in the last four days!'

Rex pulled on his T-shirt. 'Why should it start happening so much just now?'

'Maybe you're getting like Doctor Jekyll,' said Michael. 'He kept turning into Mr Hyde, and after a bit he couldn't turn himself back. You're turning into a dog more and more . . .'

Rex gave him a horrified look. 'You mean, one day it will be permanent? A dog all the time?'

'Look,' said Michael, 'if it does happen, there'll always be a cardboard box for you in our garden. I want you to know that.'

Mr Thomas tapped on the door and came in. 'Sorry to interrupt. I just wanted to tell you that we're going to see Great-Aunt Sarah on Sunday. She's asked us to lunch.' He turned to Michael. 'Why don't you come as well? I think you'd enjoy it. She's a grand old girl – taught me to play cricket.'

'Right, I'll ask Mum. Thanks, Mr Thomas.'

Mr Thomas went back downstairs.

Michael looked at Rex. 'If you're going to spend most of your time as a dog, I thought you might like someone around to look after things.'

Rex nodded gloomily. 'The way things are going, I'll need all the help I can get.'

Rex managed to stay human for the car journey, but by the time Mr Thomas pulled up outside Great-Aunt Sarah's cottage, he was already starting to itch.

They got out of the car and Great-Aunt Sarah, a sweet-looking white-haired old lady, came out to greet them. She led them straight through the cottage, through the open french windows and on to a handsome patio overlooking a beautiful flower garden.

'Wow!' said Michael.

'It's very impressive, isn't it?' said Mr Thomas. 'Rex has seen it all before, of course, haven't you, Rex . . .' He looked around, before realizing that Rex was no longer with them. 'Now where's he gone?'

'It's all right, Mr Thomas,' said Michael. 'I'll go and find him.'

Michael darted back indoors, leaving Mr Thomas apologizing for Rex's bad behaviour.

'I'm sorry, Auntie, he's such an odd boy at times.'

Great-Aunt Sarah led him to some garden chairs and they sat down. 'He's always seemed quite normal to me.'

'Normal? The other day he walked all the way

home from town in his swimming trunks. He takes *all* his clothes off sometimes.'

Great-Aunt Sarah smiled. 'I remember a boy who took all his clothes off at a cricket match.'

Mr Thomas blushed. 'That was different, Auntie. I was eighteen and it was on my birthday! Rex took them all off in the shop!'

'Not in front of the customers, surely?'

'I don't think so . . . I asked him to keep an eye on the shop for a moment, and when I came back I found his clothes in a pile on the floor and a customer being served by the dog!'

'This is the dog you told me about in your letter, is it? The one who can turn on the TV and work the video?'

'Yes . . . mind you, he watches some awful rubbish.'

Great-Aunt Sarah nodded thoughtfully. 'Yes . . . You stay here and I'll get us all something to drink.'

She got up and went into the house.

In the living room of the little cottage, Rex, now a dog again, was hiding behind the sofa. Michael was hiding Rex's clothes behind the long curtains.

'As soon as you change back, you can get dressed and come out and join us, okay?'

'Woof!'

'I'll tell them you weren't feeling well and had to lie down.'

'Woof! Woof!'

'No, they'd want to come and see you. I'll say you're in the toilet.'

'Woof! Woof!'

'Quite right, you could stay like this for hours. Don't worry, I'll think of something.'

Great-Aunt Sarah called from the kitchen. 'Have you found Rex yet, Michael? Is he all right?'

'He's fine, thank you, Mrs Griffiths.'

Michael went out into the hall, where he met Great-Aunt Sarah carrying a tray of soft drinks.

'Rex has gone for a walk,' he said. 'The car ride gave him a headache and he needed some fresh air.'

'I see,' said Great-Aunt Sarah. 'Take this tray into the garden for me will you, Michael? I'll start bringing out the food.'

'Great!' said Michael. He took the tray out on to the patio.

As soon as he was gone, Great-Aunt Sarah went into the living room. She looked keenly around and soon spotted a bit of Rex's sweater sticking out from under the curtains.

'We seem to have a bit of a problem here, don't we, Rex?'

There was no reply.

'I quite understand your not wanting to talk about it,' Great-Aunt Sarah went on. 'We'll all be in the garden having lunch, and we'll be happy to see you whenever you can join us.' She paused in the door-way. 'If there's anything you want, bowl of water, plate of food, just bark! And you will be careful about putting your paws on the furniture, won't you?'

She went out of the room. Rex emerged from behind the sofa, and sat looking after her, his head on one side.

Great-Aunt Sarah had provided an excellent salad lunch, with a delicious summer pudding to follow. As Michael spooned the last of his pudding off his plate,

Great-Aunt Sarah said, 'Will you do something for me, Michael?'

'Yes?'

'That wart on your nose . . .'

'I hoped you hadn't noticed . . .'

'It's all right, Michael,' said Mr Thomas. 'Auntie just wants you to sell it to her.'

Michael gave him an astonished look. 'Sell it?'

'I collect them, you see,' said Great-Aunt Sarah. 'I keep them in this little bag.' She showed him a leather pouch. 'And I pay cash for them.' She produced a coin. 'Fifty pence. How about it?'

'Take the money,' Mr Thomas whispered. 'Take the money!'

Michael touched the wart. 'How can I give it to you? It's on my nose. It's grown there!'

'Let me worry about that. Is it a deal?'

'I suppose so.'

Great-Aunt Sarah reached out to Michael and gently touched his nose, as if taking the wart. She seemed to put it in her leather bag and then she pushed the fifty-pence piece towards him. 'Thank you.'

Michael rubbed his nose. 'But it's still there!'

Great-Aunt Sarah smiled. 'Oh no, that's just a bit of dead skin. It will go very soon. I've got the wart!'

Rex suddenly appeared at the french windows.

Mr Thomas frowned. 'Really, Rex, where on earth have you been? You can't arrive in someone's house and just wander off . . .'

Great-Aunt Sarah touched his arm. 'It's all right, there's no harm done. Come and have some lunch, Rex, there's still some left.'

Rex sat down beside her and she filled him a plate.

She turned to Mr Thomas. 'Did you bring the cricket things down? I thought we might have a game on the lawn.'

Mr Thomas nodded. 'I'll get the bag from the car.'

'Do you think he'll be able to manage on his own, Michael?' Great-Aunt Sarah asked gently.

Michael jumped up. 'I'll give him a hand. That bag looked pretty heavy when he was loading it into the car.' He hurried off after Mr Thomas.

Rex went on eating his salad. He looked up, to find Great-Aunt Sarah watching him.

'How long has this been going on, Rex?' she asked gently.

'About a year.'

'Fun, is it?'

'Well, sometimes, but ... Great-Aunt Sarah, how did you know?'

She smiled. 'It wasn't difficult. When your father started talking about heaps of clothes around the house and a clever dog that appeared from nowhere ... It's happened before, you see. To a friend of mine.' She looked around. 'I brought down a photograph album that might interest you. Now, where did I put it?'

Rex spotted the leather-covered album on a bench close by and handed it to her. She riffled through the pages. 'Yes, here we are!' She showed him an old black-and-white photograph of a boy, a girl and a dog sitting on a beach.

Rex peered at the young man's face. 'That's Dad!'

'That's right. And that's your mother. They met on holiday.' She pointed. 'And this is the friend I was telling you about.'

'The dog?'

Great-Aunt Sarah nodded. 'She had a few adventures, I can tell you. Maybe she still does. That's how I guessed what had happened to you.' She looked keenly at him. 'There's some sort of problem, isn't there?'

Rex explained how the changing into a dog had become so much more frequent recently. 'I've been worrying that one day I'll change and never change back.'

'Have you been ill recently?' Great-Aunt Sarah asked.

'Well, I had a bit of a virus infection.'

'Did it give you a temperature?'

'Yes, it did, actually.'

'Well, I expect that's all it is,' said Great-Aunt Sarah reassuringly. 'My friend said that if you got hot, you were much more likely to change.'

'And I've had a temperature!' said Rex. 'Do you think that's all it was?'

'I'm sure of it.'

Rex beamed at her. 'That's such a relief!' He pointed to the album. 'Can I keep that photograph?'

'Of course. Here, I'll take it out for you.' She detached the photograph from the album and gave it to him. 'Now, we'd better go and play cricket with your father.'

Rex's face fell. 'I'm not too keen on cricket.'

'That's scarcely the point, is it?' said Great-Aunt Sarah gently. 'When your father asks you to play cricket, he's really saying, let's spend some time together.'

'I thought he just liked bowling.'

'It's the same as when I asked your friend to help with the cricket bag,' she explained. 'I was really saying, "Would you mind leaving us alone so I can talk to Rex?"'

Rex was astonished. 'You were?'

Great-Aunt Sarah passed him a plate of summer pudding. 'People often say the most important things under the actual words, Rex. Tell me, have you ever seen your father do his trick with the ten-pence piece?'

The trick with the ten-pence piece was pretty spectacular.

They all stood around the cricket pitch that had been set up on Great-Aunt Sarah's lawn.

'It's a long time since I've done this,' said Mr Thomas. 'I'm not sure I still can.'

'Of course you can,' Great-Aunt Sarah said firmly. She handed Rex a ten-pence coin. 'You can put it anywhere you like within five feet of the stumps. I should put it out of line a bit, so he has to put a spin on it.'

Rex put the coin five feet in front of the wicket and a little off-centre.

'Off you go!' said Great-Aunt Sarah, and Mr Thomas strode off to the bowling end. 'He has to hit the coin and then the stumps,' Great-Aunt Sarah explained. 'We used to put bets on it when he was younger.' She raised her voice. 'Ready when you are!'

Mr Thomas concentrated for a moment, then thundered up to the line and bowled. Crouching close to the stumps, Rex saw the ball land smack on the coin and then spin off to the left, to clip the bails clean off the wicket.

'Wow!' said Michael, and everyone cheered and clapped.

Mr Thomas came walking back.

'I didn't know you could do that, Dad,' Rex said admiringly.

'I wasn't entirely sure myself!'

'Well done, dear,' said Great-Aunt Sarah. 'Why don't you do it again?'

Mr Thomas shook his head. 'I think I'll quit while I'm ahead. Anyone for a game?'

They had a splendid game of cricket that took up most of the afternoon. Great-Aunt Sarah kept wicket, wearing all the proper gear, Mr Thomas did some spectacular bowling, and even Rex and Michael got in a few good whacks at the ball.

After the game, Great-Aunt Sarah served a splendid high tea. Then Mr Thomas dozed happily in a garden chair, while Rex and Michael practised bowling at ten-pence coins.

Mr Thomas woke up with a start, peered at his watch and jumped to his feet. 'Rex! Michael! Time to go! Pack the cricket things in the bag, will you? I'll take the tea things in and tell Great-Aunt Sarah we're off.'

When all the gear was loaded into the bag, Rex and Michael carried it round to the car between them.

'You know when Great-Aunt Sarah asked you to help Dad with the cricket bag,' said Rex. 'Did you know she was really saying, "Please leave us alone so I can talk to Rex"?'

'Of course I did. And when I said I'd give him a hand, I was really saying, "I am very happy to do anything for the woman who got rid of my wart!"'

'Great-Aunt Sarah got rid of your wart?'

'She bought it for fifty pence and put it in this little leather bag.' Michael touched his nose. 'It's gone!'

Mr Thomas came out of the cottage reading a note.

Michael rushed up to him. 'Mr Thomas, my wart's gone! Can I go and show Mrs Griffiths?'

'Better not disturb her, Michael. She left this note saying she'd got a bit over-heated playing cricket and had to go for a little lie-down.' He read from the note. 'She says, "Lovely to see you, safe journey home, come again soon!"'

He helped Rex lift the cricket bag into the car, then closed the boot.

'You know that thing with the ten-pence coin, Dad,' said Rex. 'Will you teach me how to do it?'

'You really want to learn?'

'Yes, I do.'

Mr Thomas looked pleased. 'Then of course I will.'

Michael looked back towards the house. 'I didn't know she had a dog.'

Rex turned and saw an old dog sitting on the porch at the front of the house.

'Goodness, I didn't think she was still alive,' said Mr Thomas. 'Her name's Alice. She must be incredibly ancient by now. Auntie's had her for years. Right, everyone into the car.'

Mr Thomas and Michael got into the car, but Rex stood still, staring at the old dog. There was something familiar about it. Then he realized: it was the dog in the old black-and-white photograph.

An incredible thought came into Rex's mind. Suddenly he just had to know. He walked over to the porch and knelt beside the dog. 'Great-Aunt Sarah?' he whispered.

The old dog lifted her head and said, 'Woof!'

Doggy Business

It was lunchtime at Oakwood Middle School. In a quiet corner of the playground, a strange scene was taking place.

Michael Tully was sitting on a bench, an open notebook on his lap. On one side of him was a large open kit-bag, on the other a small shaggy dog. In front of him was a short queue of schoolkids.

Michael took a towel out of the kit-bag and handed it to the boy at the head of the line, taking a silver coin in exchange. He put a tick in the notebook. The next customer, a girl, was given a gym shoe, and the last, a small boy called Denzil, got a sock.

Michael made a final tick in his notebook and looked up, only to see a burly boy called Simon looming over him.

'You Michael Tully?' Simon growled. 'They say your dog can find things, that right?'

'It's his nose, you see,' Michael explained. 'If he just gets a sniff of something . . .'

'Could he find my football shirt? Someone's nicked it from the changing room. I need it, we've got a match this afternoon.'

Wondering who'd be daft enough to pinch anything from someone as massive as Simon, Michael stood up. 'All right, we'll see what we can do.' He turned to the dog. 'Is that okay?'

The little dog said, 'Woof!'

'That's where it was hanging,' said Simon. 'Right there!' He pointed accusingly at an empty peg.

Michael looked along the row of lockers. 'Okay, we'll just let him get the feel of the place.'

The dog jumped up on the bench by the peg and began sniffing around.

'Someone probably forgot their own shirt and took yours,' said Michael. 'Don't worry, he'll track it down. Ah, here we go!'

The little dog jumped off the bench and began following an invisible trail along the ground. He reached the door and stood waiting for someone to open it.

Michael opened the door, and he and Simon followed the dog along the corridor until it stopped outside another door near by.

'In here?' Michael asked.

'Woof!'

'That's the girls' changing room,' said Simon.

Michael looked down at the dog. 'You're sure about this?'

'Woof!'

Michael looked at Simon and knocked on the door. 'Anyone mind if we come in?'

There was no reply.

Cautiously Michael opened the door and they all went inside. The place was pretty well identical to the boys' changing room: rows of lockers with benches underneath. It appeared to be empty.

The dog trotted along the length of the room and disappeared round the corner. There was a sudden chorus of barking, and a female scream.

Michael and Simon ran round the corner and discovered a pretty girl sitting on a bench and repairing a torn football shirt with needle and thread. The little dog sat at her feet. At the sight of the boys it gave another triumphant 'Woof!'

'Melanie!' said Simon.

'Simon!' said the girl. 'What are you doing in here?'

'What are you doing with my football shirt?'

Melanie blushed. 'I noticed that it got torn yesterday, in football practice. I just wanted to help.'

Simon too went scarlet. 'You did?' He sat down on the bench beside her and took her hand. 'Oh, Melanie!'

'Oh, Simon!'

Michael looked down at the dog. 'Oh ... Good grief!'

This last exclamation was caused by the sudden appearance of Mrs Jessop.

'What exactly is going on here?'

No one replied.

Mrs Jessop surveyed the romantic scene with a beady eye. 'Well? I'm waiting for an explanation.'

Michael sat down on a bench and put his head in his hands.

The dog sank to the ground, covering its eyes with its paws.

Mrs Jessop was sitting at her desk in her new Vice Principal's office. Michael and the dog were on the carpet in front of her.

Mrs Jessop tapped her desk with a ruler. 'You're running a business?'

'Woof!' said the dog.

Mrs Jessop read from the notebook in front of her. '"Dogsbody Enterprises"?'

Michael nodded. 'We find things for people. Well, the dog does. When you came in, he'd just found Simon's football shirt.'

'I see,' said Mrs Jessop. 'Well, I'm afraid it's got to stop.'

The dog whined and Michael said, 'But why, miss?'

'Because this is a school, not a market place. That dog isn't even supposed to be in the building!'

'But miss, in assembly you said business enterprise was a vital educational experience.'

'Never mind what I said in assembly! In future you'll have to demonstrate your business enterprise off school premises, is that understood?'

'Yes, miss.'

Michael looked so miserable that Mrs Jessop said, 'Why don't you talk to Rex's father? He runs his own business.'

'Right, miss.'

'And stay away from the girls' changing room in future,' Mrs Jessop added. 'That's not the sort of vital educational experience I had in mind!'

Unfortunately, Rex's father was tied up in a meeting with a salesman from a security company, so Rex and Michael decided to try the local library. By now Rex was back in his boy shape again.

It was a daunting experience. They sat at a table surrounded by books with titles like *The Easy Way To Set Up Your Own Business* and *Business Management Made Easy*.

The trouble was, they weren't easy at all. They were so full of jargon the boys couldn't understand them.

To make matters worse, Rex wasn't concentrating. He was worrying about his father's new security scheme. 'He's talking about putting proper locks on all the doors *and windows*.'

'So? I still don't see what you're so worried about.'

'Michael, my bedroom window is how I get in at night when I'm a dog! It's how I get to my clothes, how I reach somewhere warm and dry.' Rex started scratching agitatedly.

'So we work out some other way for you to get in. It's not that serious, is it? Not like turning into a dog in the middle of a public library.' Michael looked under the table where a small shaggy dog was sitting on a pile of clothes. 'Come on, move your paws.'

He grabbed the clothes and stuffed them in his school bag, then picked up the book Rex had been reading.

'This one any good?'

'Woof! Woof!'

'Take it back then, I'll try one of the others.'

The dog took the book gently between its teeth and trotted off to the 'Business' section.

At a table in the nearby 'Dogs' section, a middle-aged man was sitting, surrounded by a selection of books on Obedience Training. He looked up in some surprise as a small shaggy dog trotted round the corner of the book stacks and returned a book to the shelves. The dog studied the rows of books, chose another one, and went back the way it had come, the book held carefully in its mouth.

A few minutes later, the man heard a boy's voice from the other side of the stack. 'This one's no good either, much too complicated. We need something simple, a basic guide. Can't you find something like that?'

After a moment the dog reappeared. It stood looking at the books on the lower rows of the Business section, a baffled expression on its hairy face.

The man stood up and went over to the book stack. From one of the higher shelves he took a book called *The Simple Man's Guide To Setting Up A Business*. He bent down and offered it to the dog. The dog took the book and disappeared round the corner. The man returned to his studies.

Then the boy's voice came again. 'Ah now, that's more like it. Well done!'

The man got up and went round the corner. He found the dog and a boy sitting at a table with their heads together, both studying the book he'd suggested.

'Excuse me,' the man said politely. 'Is that your dog? He's rather clever, isn't he?'

'Not too bad. He still needs someone to turn the pages.'

The man noticed the notebook which lay open on the table.

'"Dogsbody Enterprises",' he read out loud. '"You've lost it. Our dog can find it!" You're setting up a business?'

'Trying to.'

The man took out his wallet and produced a business card.

'My name's Pardoe, Alex Pardoe.' He handed Michael the card. 'Now have a word with your parents or your teacher first, but if they say it's all right, give me a ring and come out and see me. "Dogsbody Enterprises" could be just what I'm looking for.'

*

Michael and Rex were in Mrs Jessop's office again, though by this time Rex was a boy again. She was studying the business card. 'Alex Pardoe. Well, well, well!'

'Do you know him, miss?' Rex asked.

'I've heard of him. You know that new industrial complex on the other side of the river? Alex Pardoe owns it. How did you two come across him?'

'In the library, miss,' Michael replied. 'He wants our dog to work for him.'

'Doing what?'

'We don't know,' said Rex. 'He just said, if you thought it was all right we should fix up to go out and see him.'

'Do you think it would be all right, miss?' Michael asked.

Mrs Jessop considered. 'I should think so. Got a day off on Thursday, haven't we? If you like, I'll drive you out there myself. I'm rather curious to know what he wants.'

'How much do you think we should charge?' Michael asked as they left the office. 'I mean, this Pardoe's obviously loaded. I think we should ask for at least two pounds an hour. If it's something extra dangerous, like taking on the Mafia, we'll insist on an extra fifty pence. What do you think, Rex?'

'I think you'd better let Mrs Jessop do the talking . . .'

The new industrial complex was housed in a huge glass building, with 'Pardoe Electronics' emblazoned across the front.

Mrs Jessop, Michael and Rex, who was now a dog again, were shown up to a hi-tech modern office on the top floor, where Mr Pardoe was waiting for them. As Michael introduced Mrs Jessop, Rex cocked his head at the sight of a handsome red setter, lying in a dog basket in the corner.

'I'm very grateful to you and er, Bob, for coming out here, Michael. And to you, Mrs Jessop, for bringing them. I'll get straight to the point. I have a problem – it's Tess here.'

The red setter pricked up her ears at the sound of her name.

'There's something wrong with her,' Mr Pardoe went on.

Mrs Jessop frowned. 'Don't you need a vet?'

'She's perfectly, healthy – but she isn't happy!'

'How do you know?' Michael asked.

'If she was happy, she wouldn't keep running away, would she?'

Mr Pardoe explained that he'd moved house to be near his new industrial complex. Almost immediately Tess had started running away. He'd begun bringing her into the office in case she was lonely, but she still disappeared at the first opportunity and she didn't come back for hours. Mr Pardoe was afraid that one day she wouldn't come home at all.

'Where does she go?' Michael asked.

'I've no idea. I've tried following her, I even hired a private detective, but you can't keep up with her.'

'You want the dog to find out where she goes to?' Mrs Jessop asked.

Mr Pardoe nodded. 'That's what I was hoping, yes. He seemed such a clever dog when I saw him in the library.'

Mrs Jessop turned to Michael. 'Do you think he could do it?'

Michael looked at the dog – who gave a confident 'Woof!'

'I think we could give it a try,' said Michael.

Mrs Pardoe was behind the wheel of her car. The boy and the dog stood by the window. Michael was holding a mobile phone.

'Now you're sure you'll be all right?' she asked.

'We'll be fine, miss,' said Michael. 'We're only going to follow a dog, after all.'

'Well, be careful. And if there's any problem, you've got Mr Pardoe's mobile phone. Just give me a call. Right?'

'Right, miss.'

As Mrs Jessop drove away, the mobile phone started ringing.

Michael listened for a moment, then said, 'Yes, got it. Okay.' He turned to the dog. 'That was Mr Pardoe. He deliberately left his door open and Tessa's disappeared. She should be coming out at any moment. Ready, Rex?'

'Woof!'

'Our first professional engagement,' said Michael. 'We've got to get this one right. This could make our reputations.'

Since he wasn't looking at the building, Michael didn't see the red setter streak down the front steps. Luckily Rex did and immediately took off after her.

Michael looked after the two fast-disappearing doggy forms.

'Okay, Rex, I'm right behind you!'

He began to run . . .

The red setter led them on an incredible chase. As she

sped across the open waste ground that surrounded the complex, they nearly lost her straight away. The red setter moved at an amazing speed, leaving Michael further and further behind. Eventually he collapsed, panting, on a heap of bricks, watching helplessly as Tessa and Rex disappeared into the distance.

'Good luck, Rex,' he gasped. 'Now it's up to you.'

Even the four-legged Rex had trouble keeping up – but once they left the wasteland and got into town, the chase became easier. Tessa, obviously a well-trained dog, trotted sedately along the busy streets, using traffic lights and zebra crossings whenever she had to cross a road. It soon became obvious that she knew just where she was going.

Rex trailed her at a discreet distance, keeping as far behind as he could without losing her. Eventually Tessa turned into a quiet suburban street. She bounded over a garden gate and sat down on the front doorstep, barking loudly.

A sweet-looking, little old lady opened the door, fussing over Tessa like an old friend. They went inside the house, leaving the door ajar.

Rex lifted the latch on the gate with his paw and slipped quietly into the house.

He found himself in a spotlessly clean hall with a strong smell of furniture polish. He could hear a voice coming from the end of the hall and crept silently towards it.

He peeped round the edge of the door and saw the old lady and Tessa in a gleaming kitchen. The red setter was watching with keen interest as the old lady emptied a can of dog food into a bowl standing ready on the work surface.

'When I've finished my shopping, we'll go for a walk by the river,' the old lady was saying. 'But you'll have to have a bath if you get all muddy. Can't let you go back to Mr Pardoe all dirty, can we?' She picked up the dog bowl. 'Come along, you can eat this in the garden.' She went out through the back door, with Tessa close behind her.

Rex turned to leave – and then noticed a telephone in the hall. It stood on a little table with a chair beside it. He jumped on to the chair, lifted the receiver with his teeth, and laid it on the table. There was a wooden pencil on the table and, after a bit of fumbling, the little dog managed to pick it up. Using the end of the pencil, he began to dial . . .

Michael was sitting on his pile of bricks, wondering what to do next when his mobile phone started ringing.

'Yes?'

'Woof!'

'Rex! Did you find out where Mr Pardoe's dog goes?'

'Woof!'

'Great! I can't believe this is really working. Hang on, I'll get the map.' Fishing a map out of his pocket, Michael spread it out. 'Now, are you north of the bypass?'

'Woof! Woof!'

'South, okay. Are you to the east of the river?'

It took a lot of questions and a lot of 'Woofs!', but finally Michael managed to narrow Rex's position down to one or two streets. Picking up his bag, he set off.

*

Michael walked along the quiet suburban street, wondering if he'd misread Rex's signals. 'Rex!' he called. 'Rex, are you there?'

'Keep your voice down, will you?' someone hissed crossly.

Michael looked around to see where it was coming from. There seemed to be no one in sight.

'Over here!'

Michael followed the sound and spotted Rex's face peering out through a garden hedge.

'Where's Tess, then?'

'In there.' Rex nodded towards the house behind him. 'A little old lady's got her.'

'Right,' said Michael, relieved it wasn't the Mafia after all. 'I think the first thing is to cut off her escape.'

'Michael, I think the first thing is to give me my clothes . . .'

'Clothes, right,' Michael said, unzipping his bag.

'And the next thing is, you call in the heavy mob.'

'What?'

'Ring Mrs Jessop!'

Meanwhile back at the sports shop the new security plan was almost complete. Mr Thomas looked up as a cheerful-looking man in overalls came down from the flat.

'Everything going all right, Mr Sullivan?'

'Just fitting the window locks now. Only . . .' Mr Sullivan sounded rather embarrassed.

'What's the problem?'

Mr Sullivan fished a crumpled sheet of paper out of his overall pocket. 'I found this note on your son's bedroom window . . .'

Mr Thomas read out the note. '"Please only fit a

lock to this window that will open when I am out.
When I am in it can be closed but it has to be open
when I am out so I can get in."'

'I'm not quite sure what sort of lock he has in
mind,' said Mr Sullivan.

Mr Thomas sighed. 'Just fit an ordinary lock, Mr
Sullivan . . .'

The suburban street was still as quiet as ever. The
only difference was that now Mrs Jessop's car was
parked opposite the old lady's house. Michael and
Rex were sitting on the wall beside it, waiting.

Rex scratched his nose. 'She's been in there for ages.
Do you think she needs help?'

Michael shook his head, staring hard at the front
door.

'I'd back Mrs Jessop even if it *was* the Mafia. If
anyone needs help, it's your little old lady! Hang on,
someone's coming out.'

The front door opened and Mrs Jessop emerged,
holding Tessa on a lead. The little old lady followed,
and the two chatted in friendly fashion for a moment.
Both were smiling.

'She's got the dog!' said Michael, turning to Rex.
He jumped backwards. 'I wish you'd warn me when
you're going to do that!'

Beside him, a small shaggy dog was sitting on a pile
of clothes. Wearily Michael grabbed them and shoved
them back in his bag.

Mrs Jessop said goodbye to the little old lady and
crossed the road.

'Everything all right, miss?' Michael asked.

'Oh yes! I should have realized what the problem
was as soon as Mr Pardoe mentioned moving.' She

pointed. 'He used to live in that big house there, right next door to the old lady, Mrs Reynolds. Every day he used to go off and leave the dog alone – he'd given Mrs Reynolds a spare key in case of emergencies. Every day Mrs Reynolds used to come round, take Tessa for walks and generally make a fuss of her. Then she'd sneak her back just before Mr Pardoe got home.'

Michael bent down and stroked the setter. 'No wonder she didn't mind being left. But then Mr Pardoe moved! Suddenly poor Tessa was really alone all day, and she didn't like it. So she started busting out and coming back here.'

'You did a good job sorting this one out,' said Mrs Jessop. 'Where's Rex, by the way?'

Michael groaned. When Mrs Jessop had arrived, she'd wanted to know why Rex the boy was there and the dog was missing. Michael had told her the dog had wandered off while he was calling Rex on Mr Pardoe's mobile phone, asking him to come over and help.

'Rex got hungry, miss,' said Michael. 'He went off to look for a café or a sweet shop. Still, at least Bob's come back.'

Mrs Jessop looked at her watch. 'I really ought to be getting back. And I wanted to take Tessa back to Mr Pardoe. He'll be worrying about her.'

'You go, miss,' said Michael. 'I'll wait here for Rex.'

'Okay, if that's what you want. I'll let you know what Mr Pardoe says tomorrow. I imagine he'll be very pleased.'

Loading Tessa into the back of her car, Mrs Jessop drove away.

Michael looked down at the dog. 'Got any fare money?'

'Woof! Woof!'

'No, neither have I. Come on!'

They started the long walk home.

'Three miles!' said Michael when they finally got to Rex's door. 'I cannot believe I actually walked three miles!'

'Woof!'

'I suppose you'll go indoors in your usual way?'

'Woof!'

'Okay, I'll call for you round the front.'

'Woof!'

Rex jumped on to the dustbin, ran along the wall, leapt on to the extension roof and jumped up at his bedroom window. It was closed. Worse still, it was locked as well. He could actually see the gleaming new window lock.

Sadly Rex turned and retraced his steps.

Michael rang the bell stood waiting by the front door until Mr Thomas appeared. 'Afternoon, Mr Thomas, I've come to see Rex.'

'He's out, I'm afraid, Michael. I'll tell him you called. You'll have to excuse me, I'm a bit busy with the new security system.'

The front door slammed. Michael heard a whine at his feet and looked down to see a sad-looking little dog. 'Window locked already?'

'Woof!'

'You were right, Rex,' said Michael. 'Your dad's new security system is going to be a real problem!'

As the boy and dog walked away, it began to rain.

Next day in her office Mrs Jessop told them how

delighted Mr Pardoe had been with their solution of the Tess mystery.

'The old lady's not going to get into any trouble, is she?' Rex asked.

'Certainly not. From now on, Mrs Reynolds will be looking after Tess officially, and getting paid for it. She's very pleased. So is Mr Pardoe. He asked me how much Dogsbody Enterprises charged. I had to say I didn't know.'

'We used to charge ten pence,' said Rex, 'ten pence for each item found.'

'I think it should be more for finding Tess,' said Michael. He looked accusingly at Rex. 'There was a lot of walking involved.'

'I think Mr Pardoe is planning to pay rather more than ten pence,' said Mrs Jessop. 'He said hiring a detective had cost him two hundred and fifty pounds, and that Dogsbody Enterprises was worth much more.'

'Two hundred and fifty pounds!' said Michael.

'Just take what he offers you, all right?' said Mrs Jessop.

'Atishoo!' said Rex.

'That's a nasty cold you've got there, Rex,' said Mrs Jessop.

'Two hundred and fifty pounds,' said Michael wonderingly, as they left the office.

'I don't want money from Mr Pardoe,' said Rex.

'You don't?' said Michael.

'Atishoo!' said Rex. 'No, there's something I need much more.'

Michael and the shaggy little dog were both sitting on chairs in Mr Pardoe's office.

'Come in, Henry, come in!' Mr Pardoe called out, holding open the door. A white-coated technician appeared, wheeling a window unit mounted on a little platform in front of him. The window was exactly like the one in Rex's room. It was even fitted with the same kind of lock.

'Well, I think we've solved your problem,' said Mr Pardoe. 'This is the type of window lock you're concerned about?'

'Woof!'

'I think so,' said Michael.

'Well, it may look the same, but Henry here has made a few alterations in our workshop. Ready, Henry?'

Henry made a few final adjustments and stepped back. 'Ready, Mr Pardoe.'

Mr Pardoe beamed. 'Now, Michael, can you get your dog to walk right up to the window and bark?'

'Okay!' Michael looked at Rex. 'Like to give it a go?'

The dog jumped down off its chair and went up to the window. 'Woof!'

The window lock clicked and the window swung open.

'Wow!' said Michael

'Not bad, is it,' Mr Pardoe said proudly. 'Now, all the dog's got to do is get inside.'

The dog sprang through the open window, landing on the other side of the frame.

'Voice-activated, you see,' said Mr Pardoe. 'Specifically set to your dog's vocal signature, so no one else can open it.'

'Amazing!' said Michael.

'Once he's inside, all he has to do is bark twice and

the signal reverses. I don't know if you can train him to do that?'

'Woof! Woof!' said the dog.

The window closed itself, and the lock clicked shut.

'He picks up things very quickly, doesn't he?' said Mr Pardoe.

Michael was lost in admiration. 'This is fantastic, Mr Pardoe. It's exactly what we wanted, it really is. Thank you!'

'Woof!' the dog agreed.

'I'd just better show you how to fix the lock to your bedroom window,' said Mr Pardoe. 'Henry, where's that screwdriver?'

The dog trotted up to him with the screwdriver in its mouth.

'That really is a very remarkable dog!' said Mr Pardoe.

Mr Thomas carried two cups of tea into the sitting room. 'Thank you for coming by, Mrs Jessop.'

'So what's the problem?'

'I'm a bit concerned about this business scheme . . .'

'Dogsbody Enterprises?'

'Rex and Michael are very full of it at the moment, but it sounds a bit risky to me.'

Mrs Jessop smiled. 'I don't think you need worry. I can't see them coming to any real harm. They may even do some good. As a matter of fact −' She broke off, listening. 'I thought you said Rex wasn't in?'

'He's not. Nobody's in. Why?'

'Well, whoever's not in just turned on the television!'

Mr Thomas listened. The sound of a nearby television set came clearly down the hall.

Mr Thomas jumped up. 'That's impossible. I've just had a whole new security system fitted. Nobody could get in without my knowing. Nobody!'

He strode along the hall, following the sound, Mrs Jessop close behind him. The noise was coming from Rex's room.

Mr Thomas flung open the door and saw the shaggy little dog lying on Rex's bed watching television, the remote close to its paw.

The dog looked up and grinned at them.

'Woof!' it said.

BEETHOVEN'S 2nd
Robert Tine

The Newton family are quite happy as dog people. But never in a million years did George Newton think they would be puppy people.

Enter Beethoven, followed by his friend, Missy and their four St Bernard puppies. They are cuter than cute and messier than anything. None the less, just like Beethoven, George and his family quickly grow to love them all.

It's a big thing to look after so many dogs. It's an even bigger thing when there are nasty people around who want to put the puppies into breeding kennels, which means it's down to Beethoven and George to save the day!

FREE WILLY
Todd Strasser

Willy is a mighty killer whale. Jesse is an eleven-year-old runaway who never had a real home. Together they form a very special friendship.

The star attraction at an amusement park, Willy is restless and longs to be reunited with his family at sea. The park owner, however, has decided that the whale is worth more dead than alive. Can Jesse free Willy before it's too late?

THE PAGEMASTER
Todd Strasser

Richard Tyler is the world's most cautious kid. Fearful of accidents wherever he turns, Richard's greatest fear becomes reality when he gets caught in a freak thunderstorm. He crashes his bike (with extra-special safety features) and rushes for cover into his local library.

There he meets the mysterious Pagemaster who takes him into a fantasy world where books literally come to life. It's not a journey for the faint-hearted, but through it Richard develops a new confidence in himself and the world around him.

THE NIGHTMARE BEFORE CHRISTMAS
Daphne Skinner

Christmas might never be the same again!

Under the orange disc of the moon in Hallowe'en Land the creatures of the night are busy. Jack Skellington is the king of this strange world, but lately he's grown tired of the same old frights. Then by chance he discovers Christmas Town. What a wonderful place, he thinks, and what a wonderful idea if Hallowe'en Land came to visit Christmas Town.

Scary, funny and touching, this is the novel based on the film *The Nightmare Before Christmas*.

JIM UGLY

Sid Fleischman

Jim Ugly is a tough, sandy mongrel, with a large helping of timber wolf. Jake doesn't really like him, but he is all he has got left to remind him of his father, who has disappeared at Smoketree Junction.

A wild adventure begins when this unlikely pair set off across the Sierra Nevada mountains in search of Jake's father and the answers to some baffling questions come to light, like the whereabouts of the fabulous diamonds which have gone missing.

YOUR MOTHER WAS A NEANDERTHAL

Jon Scieszka

What better way to avoid doing maths homework than to take a trip (with the help of Joe's magic book) back to the Stone Age. The Time Warp Trio plan to wow their ancestors with modern inventions, like juggling balls, water pistols and Walkmans. But dinosaurs, dangerous cavewomen, tigers, earthquakes and woolly mammoths are just a few of their problems.

THE PUFFIN BOOK OF HORSE AND PONY STORIES

Edited by K. M. Peyton

The best of pony stories, classic and modern, is here in this exciting addition to *The Puffin Book of* . . . series. K. M. Peyton, the author of the *Flambards* series among many award-winning books, has been a life-long horse enthusiast, and her selection is a treat for every horse and pony lover.

Famous stories such as *Smoky* and *National Velvet* are included alongside often overlooked but no less brilliant stories like *Another Pony for Jean* by Joanna Cannan and *Jump for Joy* by Pat Smythe, making this an unforgettable read.

A DOG SO SMALL

Philippa Pearce

For months, Ben Blewitt had been thinking about dogs. Alsatians, Great Danes, mastiffs, bloodhounds, borzois . . . He had picked and chosen the biggest and the best from the dog-books in the Public Library. So imagine his disappointment when, for his birthday, Ben received not a dog but a *picture* of a dog. Ben's imagination soon got to work, though, and that's when his strange adventures began.

VIDEO ROSE

Jacqueline Wilson

Rose is a video freak. Her idea of heaven is sitting in front of the video, with a packet of marshmallows resting on her tummy. Her worst nightmare is the video breaking down – which is what happens one day. Rose's whole life is changed by a strange old man who comes to mend the video, and at the same time gives her the power to rewind and fast-forward her own life.

FLOUR BABIES

Anne Fine

When the annual school science fair comes round, Mr Cartwright's class don't get to work on the Soap Factory, the Maggot Farm or the Exploding Custard Tins. To their intense disgust they get the Flour Babies – sweet little six-pound bags of flour that must be cared for at all times.

Young Simon Martin, a committed hooligan, approaches the task with little enthusiasm. But, as the days pass, he not only grows fond of his flour baby, he also comes to learn more than he ever could have imagined about the pressures and strains of being a parent.